"What do you think you're doing?"

Vanessa had never felt more indignant in her life.

"Don't ask stupid questions," Max commanded, silencing her as his mouth came down on hers.

Vanessa had been kissed before, of course, but never like this. Against the skilled assault of his hard cynical mouth there was no defense, and Vanessa succumbed to the inevitable, her body crying out for more than just his kisses, even while her mind was warning her she was a fool. Giving herself up totally to the pleasure of his touch, she cared only that this would go on forever.

Only when he released her abruptly to ask, "Shall we go back to bed," did she find the strength to thrust him from her.

"I take it the answer is no," he said.

SUSANNA FIRTH

master of shadows

Harlequin Books

TORONTO • NEW YORK • LONDON
AMSTERDAM • PARIS • SYDNEY • HAMBURG
STOCKHOLM • ATHENS • TOKYO • MILAN

Harlequin Presents first edition September 1983
ISBN 0-373-10624-6

Original hardcover edition published in 1981
by Mills & Boon Limited

CHAPTER ONE

SHE had made a terrible mistake. She should never have allowed them to talk her into coming here tonight. It had been a kind of madness in her to give in against her own better judgment, and Vanessa recognised and cursed her own folly roughly ten seconds after she crossed the threshold of the vast, brightly lit room.

'Look, love, it's see and be seen in this business, and you know that as well as I do,' Jonathan had told her firmly. 'No one's going to beat a path to your door with the offer of fame and fortune if you spend all your time skulking inside like a frightened rabbit.'

'Maybe I don't want fame and fortune,' she defied him.

'Then you're in the wrong trade, darling.' He gave an exasperated sigh and ran a weary hand through his thinning hair. 'Don't try and sell me that one. Save it for the gossip columns where it might be a good gimmick; the shy, retiring actress who never wanted to be a star. Are you telling me that you never dreamt of your name in lights? You're a little liar if you are.'

Vanessa shrugged. 'No, I'm telling you I don't like the pitfalls that come with it.'

'And going to the party of the year is one of them, I suppose?' he said sarcastically. 'Look, it's my job to sell you to the right people, and they'll all be there tonight. But how do you expect me to help you if you won't play along with me?'

'Do go, Van.' Her sister Jill added her voice to the

argument. 'You've done nothing but mope round the flat for over a month now. It'll do you good to get out and enjoy yourself for a change.'

Enjoy herself! Vanessa's mouth curled in a bitter smile. If only Jill knew what torture it was, standing here with a plastic grin on her face, pretending that she was having a lovely time. But, in the face of that double attack, it had seemed easier to give in than to argue and hold out further. Goodness knows, she had caused everyone enough trouble recently. It had seemed tactful to try to make some kind of amends.

If only someone had thought to warn her that the first person she would recognise in that blurred mass of laughing, chattering faces would be the man whom she would have given the world, if she possessed it, to avoid. She should have realised, of course. She might have known that he would be here at what purported to be the rave-up of the year, thrown by Globe Television to celebrate the launch of their prestigious new drama series on the life and loves of Lord Byron. The famous and the would-be famous had turned up in force: giddy starlets, serious actresses, writers, influential directors, big names of yesteryear and up-and-coming talents. Twenty-five storeys high, with its breathtaking views of the London skyline, the company's penthouse suite was packed to the doors with anyone who could beg, borrow or steal an invitation.

Not that Max Anderson would need to stoop to such tricks to gain admittance. He was probably number one on the guest list when the powers-that-be had drawn it up, thought Vanessa sourly. Here as of right and all too aware of the fact. There was casual confidence in the tilt of his dark head, arrogant ease in the way he stood there as if he owned the place. He was unmistakable, even in that crush, and, with a sudden revulsion of feeling, she reacted sharply, stepping back so quickly that she almost knocked over her escort in the process. His hand came out to steady her.

'Vanessa?'

'Jonathan, *he's* here!' It was an agonised whisper.

'Who's that?' he asked absently, his mind only half on her as he scanned the room for friends of his. A leading theatrical agent, professional interest rather than pure pleasure dictated that he should attend parties like this one and he was already searching the crowd for the faces of those who had been of use to him in the past or who might owe him a favour in the future. At a party like this, with anyone who was anyone attending, there would be plenty of opportunities around.

'Max Anderson. He's over there,' she told him, and jerked her head towards the other side of the room.

She had his full attention now. 'Yes, so it is.' He stared across. 'Trust him to collar the best-looking girl in the room! Present company excepted, of course.'

Vanessa ignored the compliment. It was Jonathan's stock-in-trade to reassure his clients when he felt they needed it. 'You didn't tell me he'd be here.'

'I didn't know. They didn't think to show me the guest list for my approval. But I suppose it was to be expected.'

'Why didn't you warn me?'

'You wouldn't have come if I had,' he pointed out, patiently enough. 'And it's no reason for you to be contemplating instant flight now.'

'I wasn't,' she said, and could have bitten her tongue out. That had been her first impulse, and what was the point of denying it?

'Good.' Jonathan's voice was bland. He knew her all too well. 'There's no need to worry, you know. Half the people here will be angling for an introduction to him, so he'll have his work cut out dealing with them. You should be quite safe if you want to practise avoidance tactics.'

'If I want to!' Vanessa laughed bitterly. 'What would you do in my position? Should I make a beeline for the man and thank him politely for ruining my life?'

She spoke loudly, uncaring of who heard her, and Jonathan frowned his disapproval. 'Hardly that. But you don't have to broadcast your feelings to the entire party. It's neither the time nor the place for it.'

'Forgive me if I don't agree with you. From where I'm standing it seems exactly that,' she snapped at him. 'Don't expect me to gush over him the way everyone else will obviously do. I'd rather stick a knife in his heart! If he has one, which I very much doubt. And I've a good mind to go over and tell him as much!'

'You'll do no such thing! Look, Vanessa, calm down, will you? You're building this up beyond all proportion. He was only doing his job, after all.'

'And what about *my* job? I've got a living to earn too, you know.'

'I'm glad you've remembered. It's about time you pulled yourself together and stopped this brooding over Max Anderson. It won't get you anywhere except the scrap heap. He eats little girls like you for breakfast.'

'So I've heard. But——'

'But nothing. If you want to commit professional suicide, go ahead. I won't stop you.' Jonathan sounded annoyed. Usually the mildest of men and all too used to displays of artistic temperament, he had argued round this issue too many times in the last few weeks. 'But I'm telling you to forget it. The future is what counts. Do you think Glenda Jackson got to the top by brooding over her failures?'

'Maybe she didn't have any,' Vanessa countered mutinously.

'Of course she did.' He gave her an irritable look. 'Sometimes, darling, I wonder if you're too soft for this business. It's a tough slog to the top, you know, and what you've suffered so far is a fleabite compared with the sort of thing you might have to face in the future.'

She wasn't being fair to Jonathan and she knew it. It wasn't his fault, after all. Vanessa took a grip on herself and admitted it.

'I've been a pain in the neck recently, haven't I?' she asked him.

'Well——' he began cautiously.

'I'm sorry. I'll do my best for you, whatever it takes.' She pulled a wry face. 'But being polite to Max Anderson is beyond even my acting ability for at least the next fifty years, so don't ask the impossible, will you?'

Wisely he did not argue the point, but instead took her hand and squeezed it encouragingly. 'Good girl! I've a feeling you may be lucky tonight.'

'You always say that.'

'And sometimes I'm proved right. Come along in, we've wasted enough time already.' He propelled her firmly in the direction of the bar. 'Champagne?'

'Why not?' She accepted recklessly. 'Although goodness knows what I've got to celebrate.'

'That's defeatist talk,' said Jonathan, thrusting a glass into her hand. 'Go in and win, girl. Or at least go down fighting.'

And she felt as if she was doing just that at the moment, as she stood there with the barely touched champagne in her hand, wishing desperately that she was a million miles away. Above the chatter and laughter of hundreds of people determined to have a good time on someone else's expense account the beat of the latest pop hit pulsed urgently. Fashionable couples gyrated as the mood took them in the area that had been cleared for dancing, while strobe lights flashed with manic abandon. It was a wonderful party and the whole giddy throng was having a tremendous time.

Everyone except me, reflected Vanessa dismally. She had always hated the trivial, tinselly side of her chosen profession, the fake bonhomie and insincere praise that often passed for genuine praise and was dished out on occasions such as these. As far as possible she had avoided them.

Not that a young, struggling actress like herself got invited to such grand affairs as this every day of the week. Social gatherings in the world of provincial theatre that she had inhabited until recently were limited to the occasional wine and cheese party to boost funds and foster good relations with the local community. Then the cast of the play mingled uneasily with the town's dignitaries and heaved sighs of relief when they were allowed to escape.

Of course there had been the more raucous times after first nights, celebrations of the 'bring your own bottle' variety. They had been fun, those parties, spontaneous outpourings of relief after the evening of shared tension that they had suffered, the climax to weeks of hard slog at rehearsal. They had let their hair down and enjoyed themselves. They were young and irresponsible and nobody blamed them for it.

But this party was different. Vanessa did not know a soul here that she could count as a friend, although she had recognised quite a few famous faces. She had never felt quite so alone and isolated as among this great mass of people.

Not that anyone glancing at her would have guessed what she was going through. There was that compensation at least. Her drama school training had come to her rescue and outwardly she showed every indication of enjoying herself. It would have taken a very perceptive observer to note the strained look about her eyes and the total absence of spontaneity about her smile. And no one here cared enough for that.

'I want you to look stunning tonight, darling,' Jonathan had commanded her. 'After all, I've got my reputation to think about. I can't have people saying that my taste in women is less than impeccable. I want every man at the party envying me.'

He was trying to boost her morale, and she smiled, grateful to him for making the effort. She bit back the instinctive question, 'Are you sure you want to be seen out on the town with a failure like me?' and had laughed dutifully instead, promising not to disappoint him. As far as she knew Jonathan's eyes had never strayed from his plump, homely wife, whatever temptations had been offered him, but he liked to assume the air of a man of the world for the benefit of his clients and contacts on occasions.

She had elected to wear the most daring outfit in her wardrobe; a silky midnight blue jersey dress which matched her eyes and clung to every curve of her slender body. At the front it was deceptively simple, demure, with a high neck, but it plunged past the waist at the back, leaving exposed a tantalising expanse of creamy skin. With her jet-dark hair secured in a severe chignon that emphasised the beautiful bone structure of her face, she looked every inch a cool, sophisticated woman of the world.

'Classy.' Jonathan's voice held approval when he saw her in it. He realised how fragile that elegant veneer was, of course. But it had not kept him by her side. He knew how she felt about attending this party, about socialising at all just now. It had taken him long enough to persuade her to come with him. He had promised faithfully to look after her. 'Don't worry, love. I'll be holding your hand all evening.'

Damn Jonathan! When did he ever keep his word once he had manipulated you into doing exactly what suited his purposes for you? She should have known that it was all flannel on his part. Scarcely five minutes after they had arrived and he had done his duty by her in securing a drink for her, he had deserted her with a muttered excuse and a command that she should circulate to go to an attractive blonde who was holding court on the other side of the room. Vanessa recognised her as Charlotte Carr, whose short but glittering career in films and television she had followed with envy. She had a leading role in the Byron series and she was surrounded by people eager to congratulate her. As her agent Jonathan bathed in reflected glory at her side. And rightly so, for he was the man whose efforts on her behalf, combined with her own talent, had secured her the sought-after part. She was talking animatedly to him with a pretty air of deference that fooled nobody, least of all Jonathan, into thinking that she was modestly diffident about her success.

'Damn Jonathan!' Vanessa muttered the words aloud this time, letting her icy control slip for a second. Still, she supposed she could hardly blame him. Success was self-generating. No one wanted to be associated with a failure and, after the way she had let him down, it was good of him even to invite her here tonight. He could have taken any one of his successful clients rather than the newest girl on his books who had repaid his hard work in getting her a West End part by fouling up the whole thing.

He had picked her out when he had seen her working in a dreary Midlands repertory theatre that he had chanced to visit on the lookout for new talent. He had promised to be in touch and she had dismissed that as pie in the sky, aware of how easily such promises were broken. But Jonathan had kept his word, summoning Vanessa to London to audition for a new play.

'It's got all the right ingredients for success,' he explained to her, when she visited his small office near Shaftesbury Avenue, the heart of London's theatreland. 'If I'd tried, I couldn't have come up with a more perfect vehicle for your West End debut. The cast reads like *Who's Who in the Theatre* and the guy who wrote it has four other smash hits in town at the moment, all with sell-out audiences. If you get it, you're made, my girl.'

'*If* I get it,' Vanessa warned him, trying to strike a cautious note although everything inside her was blazing with optimism and she was already working out how to break the news to her sister Jill that she had finally made it to the big time. 'Don't expect miracles, will you?'

'You'll get it,' he told her confidently, the shrewd grey eyes taking in her excitement. 'You're good. But surely you know that?'

She disclaimed, laughing as she did so. 'Self-praise is no recommendation, Mr West.'

'Make it Jonathan—everyone else does. And remember, in this business modesty doesn't pay the rent. You should have discovered that by now. It's a tough profession. You've got to sell yourself all the time to the right people. Don't ever expect anyone else to sing your praises. They'd rather cut your throat.'

'Even a good agent like yourself?' she queried, half flattering, half serious.

'Especially a good agent like myself. I've a hundred good actresses on my books and I get my cut whichever one of them gets the part,' he said. 'Remember that, Vanessa, and you won't go wrong. A hundred actresses for every part that comes along and ninety-nine of them are prepared to tell every lie in the book about themselves so that they can clinch that part. It's the law of the jungle and, if you want to survive, don't ever forget it.'

'I won't,' she told him obediently. 'I'll do my best for you, Jonathan.'

And she had, defeating fifty other girls short-listed for the part. How she had revelled in it all! She was young, ridiculously young at twenty-two, to be starring in such an important play, and suddenly the world was her oyster. With her dark, slightly exotic looks and her naïve willingness to talk about herself and her career to any journalist who cared to take an interest in her, she was attractive enough fodder for the gossip columns. One of the last features on her before the play had opened had been a spread in one of the colour supplements. It had included a charming photograph of her, carefully posed by a flowering cherry tree in full bloom, the pale blossoms making an enchanting frame for her. 'Vanessa Herbert, the theatre's newest star, relaxes between rehearsals for her latest play, *Pontoon*.' The eyes that stared out of the picture were careless, laughingly aware of their owner's self-importance. She had learned Jonathan's lesson of never under-valuing herself all too well by that stage.

'Stupid fool!' Vanessa categorised herself, closing her eyes in sudden pain at the memory. She had been an idiot to accept as truth the flattery heaped on her, to believe the bright promises that they had all made concerning her future. Yet the play that everyone said could not fail had been a resounding flop. And she blamed herself for that almost as much as she blamed the man who had noticed her inadequacy and had blazoned it forth to the world, branding her publicly as totally lacking in talent of any kind.

The other reviewers were reasonably kind, making

light of her inexperience and sheer panic on the first
night when she had given the impression that she was
all kinds of fool by actually forgetting her lines. Some
writers had tactfully ignored her performance and
praised her looks.

But, in the world of the theatre, only one voice mattered. And Max Anderson had given the play his personal thumbs-down, viciously savaging author, director
and cast, but reserving the bulk of his sarcastic comments for Vanessa's performance in particular. It had
been a brutal attack, even for him, prompting a couple
of her friends to ask what on earth she had done to
offend the great man.

'Nothing, as far as I know,' she told them bitterly.
'Except, of course, that I dared to set foot on a stage
when, according to him, I should have taken up almost
any other career in the world.'

She wept when she read what he had to say about
her, the hot tears spilling down her cheeks as she alternately raged and acknowledged the truth of his words.

Her sister Jill whose flat she had shared since her
return to London to prepare for the play, offered a
sympathy based on a total lack of understanding of
anything theatrical and a violent partisanship of
Vanessa. In an effort to soothe, she pointed out brac-
ingly, if tactlessly, 'It's only one play, love. Don't take it
to heart. There'll be others.'

'That's what you think! They don't give you a second
chance—not ever. And particularly not when Max
Anderson's just wiped the floor with you.'

'Rubbish! Just because one man doesn't like it, it
doesn't mean the play's finished.'

Vanessa gave a watery sniff and explained patiently,
'I'm afraid it does, Jill. You just don't realise what
power that man wields. If he sees a play and decides
that he doesn't like it, they tend to put up the shutters

at the theatre the very next day.' She studied the newspaper for the umpteenth time and read again the cruel, bitingly dismissive words, unable to drag her eyes from the column that had killed her hopes for the play and her part in it. 'Look at it yourself, Jill. After that we'll be lucky to last the week out.'

'No man has that much power.'

'Oh, doesn't he? You don't know him.'

'Neither do you,' her sister pointed out reasonably enough.

'By reputation, only too well.' Vanessa pulled a face. 'He can't resist playing God and cutting us all down to size when he sees fit. And yet everyone grovels to him, hanging on his every word. It makes me sick!'

'Be fair. If he'd liked your play, you'd have been the first to praise his good taste.'

'Catch me praising anything about him!' Vanessa glowered at the small inset photograph at the head of the column that proclaimed Max Anderson at last night's play. Even in the poor newspaper reproduction she could recognise the insolent assurance in his face and the cynicism in the cruel, sensual mouth. 'He looks what he is, an arrogant swine.'

Jill considered the picture in her turn. 'I'd say he was rather good-looking.'

'Tall, dark and handsome. Just your type,' Vanessa jeered harshly. 'And he's stinking rich too. The media people are falling over each other in an effort to win his services for every feature they do on the arts. And they're welcome to him as far as I'm concerned. So are you.'

Her sister laughed. 'Out of my league, I should think. And out of yours, too, Van. If he's as influential as you say there's nothing you can do about it.'

'Do you think I don't know that? Mere mortals can't aspire to the dizzy heights that Mr Max Anderson inhabits.'

'If that's true he must lead a very lonely life.'

'There's admission to his circle for a chosen few,' Vanessa conceded. 'And there are always attractive women. He's any amount of time for them, by all accounts,' she said sourly.

'Women?' Jill was intrigued now.

'Do you never read the gossip columns? A new one every fortnight on average. They queue up for the privilege of being able to tell the world what a wonderful man he is when he chucks them over. He goes for beauty rather than brains. Predictably, I suppose. I expect his ego can't cope with intelligent women. Men like that can't bear to have their superiority challenged. It might make them insecure, and that would never do.'

'He sounds the least likely candidate for an inferiority complex of anyone that I've ever heard of.'

'As you said, not in our league,' Vanessa admitted, half envying the man his self-confidence. She could do with even a quarter of his arrogant self-conceit at the moment.

'It's just as well that you never had to tangle with him in person,' commented Jill. 'He sounds like the thinking girl's Bluebeard.'

'I'd give him a piece of my mind if I ever did meet him,' Vanessa vowed. 'He deserves to be brought to his knees by someone. And when I'd got him there I'd slap him down even further.'

'He'd be trembling in his hand-made shoes if he could hear you!'

And, reluctantly, she had seen the funny side of her tiny spear of defiance raised against the mighty Max Anderson and had joined in the laugh against herself.

It was small consolation to be proved right about the fate of *Pontoon*. Barely a week after the play had opened in such an atmosphere of hope and cheerfulness the cast was assembled and given notice to quit. Most took it philosophically. They had seen the writing on the wall with a theatre of half-empty seats and a depressing lack of advance bookings. The old hands survived flops before and came back fighting. Only Vanessa, rejected after her first real chance in the West End, found it hard to adjust, despite the good advice that she received from all around her.

'Cheer up, love, it's not the end of the world.' An elderly character actress, who had found no particular difficulty in getting another part lined up, offered consolation.

Vanessa forced herself to smile. 'That's what my sister says. But it was my big chance, that I'd spent years waiting for. And now it's come and gone so quickly that I hardly noticed it.'

'You'll get over it. You're young, there'll be other chances. Wait until you're my age and casting directors start to wonder if you'll last the distance. *Then* you can start to worry.'

She laughed, as she was meant to do, but went away quite unconvinced. Yes, she was young. And she had thought she was talented. But what use was that when the authoritative voice of Max Anderson had written, 'She attacks the part with an excess of amateurish enthusiasm, which, nevertheless, fails to disguise her lack of talent.' How could anyone be expected to pick up the pieces after that?

She had cowered indoors, refusing even to look for another job, living on her meagre savings and then on Jill's charity. She despised herself for doing it, for she had no intention of being a burden on her sister, but somehow she lacked the confidence to bounce back at the world. It had taken Jonathan days of pleading, reasoning, arguing and finally raging to make her take the first step back to normality.

And who did she see when she made that supreme

effort and dragged herself here tonight? Only the man responsible for the whole mess! She studied him dispassionately, secure that she was unobserved. *He* was far too busy with the blonde by his side, whose generous curves were spilling out of the tight silk dress in which she had encased them. Her vacant, rather doll-like features were turned adoringly towards her escort, as he bent towards her.

'Poor little sucker! Don't you know he's only got one use for you, and it's certainly not anything to do with your brilliant conversation.' Vanessa did not voice the thought, but, almost as if reacting to it, Max Anderson's head jerked upright and swung in her direction, his glance first casual, then with a sudden intentness that scared her, although she did not know exactly why.

Did every woman who caught his eye have to suffer that penetrating look as if he were stripping her, body and soul, making a ten second survey and instant judgment? Or was he just registering his annoyance that Vanessa Herbert, actress, already inspected and found wanting, should have the nerve to present herself before him for reassessment? Her chin went up in a conscious gesture of defiance and she gave him back stare for stare. A quizzical dark brow registered the fact and then, as the woman by his side claimed his attention again by tugging at his sleeve, he turned away.

Vanessa caught her breath, half relieved and half disappointed that he had been so easily distracted. For a moment it had seemed that the obvious antagonism in her expression had intrigued him in some way and would prompt him to some kind of action. Max Anderson certainly did not look the sort of man to resist a challenge, and he had acknowledged her reaction to him as just that.

She caught Jonathan's eye across the room and he gave her a look of pointed disapproval. He had obvi-

ously noted that she had been standing, as if rooted to
the spot, for a good quarter of an hour, instead of circulating in search of useful contacts as he expected her
to do. Please heaven he hadn't seen her trading silent
insults with Max Anderson. She smiled placatingly at
him.

Quickly she drained her glass and turned in search of
more champagne to bolster her morale. Although not
normally much of a drinker she had a definite feeling
that tonight some Dutch courage was in order if she
was to get through the evening ahead. At least the
worst was over—she had survived Max Anderson's blis-
tering look without too much trauma. Feeling slightly
more human, Vanessa moved towards the bar. First a
drink, then perhaps a circuit of the room. There must
be someone here that she knew, even if most of her
friends were scattered throughout England, acting at
small provincial theatres and awaiting their call to the
big time as eagerly as she had done.

'Let me get you another drink.' A firm hand closed
over hers and an attractive, low-pitched voice sounded
in her ears.

'Why, thank you——' Startled, she looked up and
broke off suddenly as she registered Max Anderson's
presence at her side.

CHAPTER TWO

Vanessa stared blankly at him.

'It was champagne, wasn't it?'

'I—oh, yes,' she managed.

He removed the empty glass from her nerveless hand and deftly exchanged it for a full one as a waiter passed by with a laden tray. He took a glass for himself at the same time.

If it had been left to Vanessa they would have stood there in total silence while she fought for control of her whirling thoughts. Had he recognised her? Surely the great Max Anderson hadn't come over to offer his apologies to her for doubting her acting abilities?

His next words quickly dispelled *that* illusion. 'You seemed surprised to see me. Didn't you think I'd respond to an invitation from the most attractive woman in the room?'

She suppressed the urge to slap his face there and then. So he had not recognised her. Not even Max Anderson would have the gall to try that gambit so confidently if he remembered how he had poured such scorn on her only a month ago. A woman slighted professionally would hardly be one to approach socially without expecting some kind of trouble. She gave an involuntary smile. Trouble, she decided, was exactly what he would get, whether he was expecting it or not.

'Invitation?' she echoed blankly, playing for time.

He laughed, the casual, assured laugh of a man who knows his way around. 'I thought I knew all the little tricks that women use to arouse a man's interest, but you certainly have a new approach.'

'Thank you,' she said demurely. There was no point in denying it. He would not believe her. And he was right, of course. Consciously or not she had wanted to intrigue him and she had succeeded all too well. But how on earth did she play it from here?

'That look was guaranteed to entice any man to your side in thirty seconds flat.'

'You think that was what I wanted—to entice you over?'

'Didn't you? It's as good a way of securing an introduction as any. And using more conventional methods you could well have waited all evening.'

Conceited devil! she thought angrily, but forced herself to be pleasant. 'Possibly. You're a very popular man, Mr Anderson.'

'You know who I am, then?'

As if he was in any doubt. 'The admiring throng alerted me to the fact. Your face is quite well known.'

He threw her a wry look. 'Television brings instant celebrity these days. Appear on the box a couple of times in whatever capacity and you're mobbed every time you venture out.'

'That must be terrible for you,' Vanessa cooed sympathetically, and wondered if she had overdone it when he shot her a quick, suspicious glance as if detecting another meaning. 'But there must be some advantages, surely?'

'A few. I get better service in restaurants nowadays, although I know what the animals in the zoo must suffer at feeding time. The great British public finds the sight of someone famous champing his way through a meal of all-absorbing interest.'

He meant her to laugh, and she obliged him. 'No other pluses?'

'Oh, the way beautiful women throw themselves at

me at parties and give every appearance of delight in
my company. That's a compensation, if you like.'

'And, being an opportunist, you naturally make the
most of it?'

'Wouldn't you, in the same position?'

'Probably,' she acknowledged. 'But, as I'll never
reach the giddy heights you occupy, it's hardly likely
that I'll have a chance to find out.' She took another sip
of champagne and asked him, 'Does it not bother you
when a woman takes the initiative?'

'Offend my male pride, you mean? Not when she's as
lovely as you are.' His eyes lingered appreciatively over
the curves that her dress emphasised rather than concealed.

'Most men like to have control of a situation.'

'Who says I don't?' he queried. 'Most *women* prefer a
man to take charge.'

'Only after a woman's shown herself willing to play
along.'

'If you like. It's all part of the game.'

'And do you enjoy playing games, Mr Anderson?'
Vanessa asked boldly.

'That depends on who my partner is.'

'I wouldn't have thought that mattered too much. If
the gossip columns are anything to go by, you change
your women the way most men change their shirts.'

There was a faintly cynical look to his well-shaped
mouth. 'Variety is the spice of life, or so they say.'

'You mean that you don't like to be tied down.'

'Perhaps. I can be led, but not coerced. When a
woman starts making too many demands on me the
parting of the ways usually comes sooner than she ex-
pects.'

'And does the reverse never apply?'

He laughed briefly. 'Not in my experience. When she
thinks she's found a meal ticket the average woman is

perfectly content to stick with him, whatever he hands out.'

'That's rather a sweeping statement.'

'But a true one, nevertheless.'

Vanessa glanced across the room and met the scorching look directed at her by the over-ripe blonde that he had deserted to come over to her. 'Well, there's one dissatisfied lady, for a start.'

'Karen? Oh, she's nothing serious and scarcely in the meal ticket class.' He looked indifferent. 'Yes, she's annoyed with me for leaving her. But as she buttonholed me when I arrived and has stuck to me like a leech ever since I think she's had a fair innings, don't you?'

'She thought she was getting somewhere, presumably?'

'And she's just got the message that she hasn't managed it. I shouldn't waste any sympathy on her. The minute something better heaves into sight, you won't see her for dust. It's inevitable, I'm afraid.'

'You're a conceited swine, aren't you?' she asked him pleasantly. 'You think you know it all.'

'Accept it. I'm right, you know. I'm afraid when it comes to trying to outmanoeuvre us your sex is boringly predictable.'

Not this member of the female sex, Vanessa thought viciously. This boringly predictable woman is going to give you the shock of your arrogant life any minute now if she can only achieve it.

'Perhaps,' she acknowledged in her turn, giving him a charmingly rueful smile. This was the way to play it, she realised now. Flirt with the man and arouse his interest as she had been doing up till now, lure him on to false hopes of an easy conquest and then slap him down in the area where, despite his protests that he was invincible, it would clearly hurt him most: his male pride.

He was trying his hand with her, assuming that she was just another empty-headed girl who wanted to meet the man of the hour. Well, she had prayed for a chance to get even with him, never expecting it to come her way. Now that it had she was going to enjoy it to the full. 'You're a shrewd judge,' she commented.

'I've had a lot of experience.'

'I can imagine, Mr Anderson.'

He frowned. 'I'm Max to my friends.'

'Do you have any?' The words were out before she could stop them.

'A few.' He glanced with faint contempt at the crowd around them. 'There aren't many here tonight.'

She deliberately misinterpreted the remark. 'If you spend most of your time pointing out other people's failings in public places, you can't really complain if they dislike you.'

'I'm a professional. I do a good job. If people don't like me they can do the other thing. I don't give a damn.'

'Most people would in your situation.'

'I'm not most people.'

'So I'd gathered. You're very sure of yourself, aren't you?'

He was finding her intriguing, she could tell. He wasn't used to a woman who answered back. He smiled down at her, that inviting, slightly world-weary smile that brought in the fan-mail by the sackful and increased the viewing figures for minority interest programmes by phenomenal amounts whenever he graced the television screens with his presence. 'It's part of my charm.'

'Like your engaging lack of self-modesty?' she ventured sweetly.

'Maybe. My virtues are many.'

'That's not what I've heard.'

'That would depend to whom you'd been talking. Or did you find that in the gossip columns too?'

'I don't want to delve into your private life. It's of no interest to me.'

'Really? Why the inquisition, then?'

Vanessa shrugged. 'I wanted to know what made a man like you tick.'

'Why? Who exactly are you? You've the advantage of me in the name stakes.' He sounded suddenly suspicious. 'You're not a journalist, are you?'

She ignored the first question and answered the second. 'Are you scared of your fellow hacks? Do you think that one day one of them will break ranks and expose you for what you really are?'

'And what am I?' he asked. She had his full attention now. She had supposed, without really considering the matter, that his eyes would be dark too. But the look he narrowed on her was tawny, green-flecked. The eyes of a predator, she thought irrelevantly. It occurred to her, rather late in the day, that Max Anderson was a dangerous man to provoke.

At the moment he was wary, nothing more. 'No, not a journalist,' he decided. 'That sharp tongue wouldn't get you very far, if you were.'

'You would know all about winning friends and influencing people, of course.'

'Of course,' he agreed easily. 'You know, I'm beginning to think you don't like me. Am I so unattractive?'

Only a man who was totally confident of the effect his looks had on women would have dared to ask a question like that. She paused for perhaps thirty seconds, then responded to his challenge.

'You're not bad-looking,' she told him casually.

'Thanks.'

She studied him carefully, registering and determinedly ignoring an involuntary pull of attraction as she did so. 'Tall, dark and handsome—I suppose that's the way most women would describe you.'

He looked politely interested. 'Yes?'

She continued listing his attributes. 'Broad shoulders, slim hips, not a spare ounce of flab anywhere, although you must be pushing thirty-five——'

'You make me sound like a prize bull being sold for stud,' he commented dryly.

'Ah, yes. That brings me to your other attributes.'

'We'll take those as listed, shall we?' he said smoothly.

If she had hoped to embarrass him she had failed dismally. Vanessa shrugged. 'If you like. I was going to add that the fact that you're fairly rich and not legally tied to another woman is presumably part of your attraction for most women.'

'But not for you?'

'That's only the outer casing, isn't it? *I'd* want something more than that in a man.'

'You don't grant me anything else?' His tone was smooth, but she was sure she was getting to him now. The muscle that twitched suddenly at the side of his mouth gave a good indication that he was having difficulty keeping his anger at bay. Max Anderson wasn't as cool as he gave out.

'You're intelligent, I'll grant you,' she shrugged.

'You're very kind.'

'You'd hardly have got to your present eminent position without some brains. You're shrewd and presumably ambitious to have got so far so soon.'

'But?'

But you're also a conceited, inconsiderate, arrogant swine. And as far as I'm concerned that cancels out any other minor virtues you might possess. Vanessa paused deliberately, savouring the moment when she finally got her own back on him for the hurt he had inflicted on her. Let Mr High and Mighty Anderson see what it was like to be rejected!

'You really do have a great opinion of yourself, don't you?' she said. 'I'm sorry if it comes as a shock to you, but I'm totally unmoved by either your fame or your oft-proclaimed attractions. To be blunt, Mr Anderson, you're just a bore. And now, if you'll excuse me, I'll——'

'No.' He anticipated her sudden movement away from him and his hand snaked out to prevent it, grasping her firmly round the waist. The sleeve of his dark evening jacket was rough where it brushed against her bare skin, and Vanessa tensed as she felt the muscled strength of the arm that imprisoned her.

'Do you usually have to use brute force to make a woman endure your company?' So much for her grand exit line. She struggled and then, realising how useless it was unless she wanted to create a scene, stood still. Max Anderson would release her in his good time, that much was clear.

'You make me sound like some kind of monster,' he said. 'Yet you don't even know me.'

'I don't want to know you,' she told him emphatically.

'That's a pity.' He jerked her closer to him. 'Because I certainly want a few more details about you. Like your name, for a start.'

She was silent. The blazing fury of the last few moments was dying down and being replaced by a sick feeling. She had burnt her boats with a vengeance now, even if she had slightly scorched Max Anderson in the process. What was it Jonathan had said about committing professional suicide?

'Well?' he prompted.

She thought furiously. Could she get away with giving him an invented name? Would he bother to check up? Or should she give up any chance of concealment and tell him bluntly who she was and why she disliked him so?

'I'm waiting,' he said nastily. 'And patience isn't one of the virtues you credited me with.'

But even as he spoke the reprieve that she was praying for arrived. A small, balding man, visibly embarrassed at having to break up what seemed to be a cosy twosome, was at Max's side, trying to attract his attention.

'Mr Anderson, I have the head of Stateside Television on the phone for you from New York.' He glanced dubiously at Vanessa, noting how closely she was clamped to Max's side, and making her feel absurdly selfconscious of the fact. 'I understand it's something rather urgent or I wouldn't have bothered you—but if you'd rather not——' His voice tailed off uncertainly.

For a moment Vanessa thought he was going to be sent packing in no uncertain terms as a look of impatience crossed Max's face. Then, obviously thinking better of the impulse, he jerked his dark head in reluctant assent. 'Yes, I'll take it.' His arm tightened fractionally round Vanessa as he told her, 'Don't think I've finished with you. If you're not here when I get back, I'll find you wherever you're hiding yourself. But if you know what's best for yourself, you won't put me to that much trouble. I'm told I can be quite dangerous when I lose my temper.'

She could well believe it. He let her go and moved away, allowing the other man to lead him in the direction of the door.

'If you'd like to take the call in my office, I'll see that you're not disturbed,' Vanessa heard the little man say as they walked off. Presumably it was a business call and it would be a lengthy one. That gave her time enough to vanish before Max Anderson returned. She had no intention of remaining meekly in the same spot so that he could resume his inquisition of her. She doubted whether he would attempt to track her down. Whatever he said there would be too many people claiming his time, including, presumably, Karen. Vanessa was sure that *she* wouldn't give up as easily as Max had thought.

To be on the safe side she would rather leave the party now, but Vanessa knew that there was no hope at all of persuading Jonathan to vanish this early in the evening. And it was hardly polite to disappear without her escort for the evening, however bad a job he had made of it so far. No, the best thing to do was just to plunge into the mass of people on the other side of the room and hope she was able to submerge herself successfully in the crowd.

She edged her way past groups of talking, laughing partygoers, intending to stand by the far wall where she might be able to watch for Max's re-entry into the room without him seeing her, but she was brought up short against a fat, red-faced man with a drink in one hand and a cigar in the other, who seemed reluctant or incapable of moving aside to let her pass.

'I'm sorry,' she apologised hastily as she almost knocked into him. 'It's a terrible crush, isn't it?'

He rescued his drink which was in danger of spilling over her dress. 'That's all right.' She saw him register her attraction and dwell upon it, very obviously liking what he saw. 'My fault for getting in your way. But no harm done, was there?' He eyed her speculatively and planted himself solidly in her path. 'It must be my lucky night.'

Vanessa smiled dubiously. She seemed to remember Jonathan pointing this man out to her as one of the notables, but she had forgotten his name. Not surprising really, after the tensions of the last few moments.

She glanced back towards the door. Still no sign of Max Anderson. Perhaps this man, whoever he was, might provide a good cover.

Fortunately he saved her the trouble of asking his name. She had discovered fairly early in her career that the famous and those who considered themselves to be so had a marked dislike of having to remind people of their identities. 'Sam Galveston, executive producer for the Byron series,' he informed her, transferring his cigar to his mouth and extending a podgy hand. 'But I expect you already knew that.'

She forced a smile. 'Of course, Mr Galveston. May I offer my congratulations on the project?' He intended her to be impressed and she played along nobly, wishing at the same time that he would let go of her hand. Still, there must be more to the man than appeared at first glance, to hold down a job like that. The television world was a jungle where only the ablest survived.

Jonathan would expect her to charm this man. Vanessa volunteered her name and then, as he seemed to be expecting them, further compliments on his work. Only one episode had been shown so far, and truth to tell, she had found it trivial and of poor quality, but she could not say so.

'I'm glad you liked it.' He beamed approvingly at her. '*He* didn't.' He jerked the cigar in the general direction of the crowded room behind them.

'Who?' Why was she bothering to ask? There was only one man whose opinions carried that sort of impact.

'Max Anderson.' He produced a much-thumbed newspaper cutting from his pocket and handed it to her. 'Ill formed, ill written and ill at ease—that's what he called it. Look for yourself. And he has the nerve to turn up here tonight. I suppose we should be grateful that he didn't choose to blast us on one of our own television programmes. I wouldn't put even that past him. And when I think what this company pays him!'

She scanned the review quickly and gave it back to him, still intent on making a good impression. 'Perhaps the viewing public will think otherwise, Mr Galveston,' she said encouragingly, without much inner conviction. She knew only too well what effect Max Anderson had upon public taste. Pithily sarcastic, the review had denounced every weakness that she had noticed in the series and a few more besides.

'The critics, for heaven's sake! What do they know about anything?' Sam Galveston growled. 'Jumped-up nobodies, full of their own importance. They don't give a damn for anybody except themselves. And Anderson's the worst of the lot!'

Vanessa could agree wholeheartedly with that sentiment at least and echoed him enthusiastically. She accepted his offer of a drink and they raised their glasses to the confusion of drama critics and of anyone else foolish enough not to appreciate their work. Suddenly the party seemed a brighter place and Sam Galveston's chubby features held a friendliness that Vanessa had not noticed before. Another glass replaced her quickly emptied one and she gave up glancing nervously behind her for Max Anderson. Who cared about the man anyway?

She downed another drink and found herself relaxing.

'So you're an actress?' Sam Galveston seemed interested and she told him a little about herself. He countered with tales of rivalries and factions within Globe Television. His jokes weren't very good, but she laughed at them. She was beginning to like this man. On his next trip back from the bar she made no objection when he took her arm and drew her towards a side-door.

'I can't hear myself think in this din,' he complained. 'And I want to tell you about my new project. I don't suppose Max Anderson will like this one, either. But who cares?'

'Who cares?' echoed Vanessa, and laughed. The earlier exhilaration of her encounter with Max had been replaced by a bright, bubbly elation that was equally stimulating. She was floating on air at the moment, the lights and the noise running into each other in a gloriously happy haze that was warm and comforting. And the man by her side, an important television producer, wanted to talk to her. That would be something to tell Jonathan, if she landed a part in Sam Galveston's next series. She must remember to be nice to the man. She slanted a wide smile in Sam's direction and he responded by squeezing her arm as he pulled her away from the main party and into a dimly lit corridor.

A slight feeling of unease invaded the warm muzziness that enveloped her. 'Where are we going?'

His arm circled her waist and she caught a sudden waft of hot, drink-laden breath as he lurched closer to her and gave a knowing laugh. 'You were hoping for a part in my new series, weren't you? You actresses are all the same—always want to talk business. Well, I've no objections, darling. But we can find something better to do than just talk, can't we?'

Her fuddled senses suddenly clanged alarm bells that should have sounded long before she got herself in this position. But somehow, weak at the knees from her encounter with Max Anderson, she had not bothered too much about any other man's motives. All men were angels compared with *him*.

'What—what do you mean?' she fenced, knowing all too well.

He drained his glass and set it down on a nearby ledge. Then his arm tightened unpleasantly about her and his free hand groped for her breasts. 'Come on now, darling, no need to spell it out. You know what I want. I'll remember you in the future, if you're nice to me now.'

Vanessa had never been the sort of girl who sold her favours on that sort of basis, although she had known many of her contemporaries do so. Although the casting couch was no substitute for talent nowadays, it sometimes made a very acceptable accompaniment to it. But she had no intention of taking that path herself, whatever the rewards offered to her. She fought to free herself, but the man seemed to have six arms. As soon as she removed his hand from one part of her anatomy she was struggling to evade his clutch elsewhere.

'Please, Mr Galveston—Sam—let me go!'

'Playing hard to get?' He gave a lecherous laugh as she freed herself from him at last and backed cautiously away. She felt slightly dizzy, whether from reaction or from the drinks he had poured down her she could not say. Her tired brain told her that if she fenced for long enough she might discourage him or at least enlist the help of someone who was leaving the party.

He was between her and the door that led back to the penthouse suite and there was no chance of side-stepping him and bolting away from danger. Desperately she edged away from him. 'Tell me about your new project, Mr Galveston,' she invited him. 'It sounds interesting. I'd like to work on it.'

He was not that easily diverted. 'Later, sweetheart. You and I have got other things to do right now. Come here, will you?'

He lunged out at her and she sprang back again, stopping short as her hands encountered a concrete post behind her. Out of the corner of her eye she registered that he had literally backed her into a corner from which there was no escape. She was up against the side of the wall and one of the wide picture windows and, short of opening it and flinging herself out, there was nothing she could do to get away.

Her adversary realised her dilemma a few seconds after it had dawned on her and gave a low laugh. 'I've caught you now,' he taunted her, and as she pressed herself against the wall, its coldness striking chill against her bare back, his hands reached out to fondle her.

Instinctively she struggled, but the twistings of her body against his seemed only to excite him further. She cried out as his hand clutched the soft material of her dress and then she felt it give and tear. His hot breath on her face repelled her and she turned her head from side to side in an effort to evade those eager, rubbery lips. How could she ever have thought that Sam Galveston was a friendly, harmless type?

'Let me go! For pity's sake, let me go,' she begged him, but he was past hearing her now, his eager hands running over the bare flesh of her shoulders and breasts, polluting them with his touch.

She was nearly fainting, past any attempt to fight him further. She screamed, but it was hopeless to think that anyone at the party would hear her with all that noise going on. Then suddenly she was conscious of the heavy weight pressing against her body being jerked away from her as a man's voice said coldly from somewhere in the background, 'I think the lady's changed her mind, Sam.' A strong hand on Galveston's shoulder spun him round with apparent ease.

'What the——?' Sam Galveston muttered something, fortunately unintelligible, then made a move back towards Vanessa. 'Let's ask the little lady about that.'

Shuddering, she cringed away from him and gave a strangled sound of protest.

'You've had your answer, I think.' The voice seemed

to come from miles away. A clear, incisive voice, accustomed to command and blessedly unfuddled by alcohol. A voice that was all too familiar, although she had heard it for the first time only that evening. 'Why not get back to the party, Sam? Plenty more there where she came from, and the night is young by your standards,' Max Anderson said coldly.

'Damn you for interfering!' The other man straightened, clearly wondering whether to try to rid himself of this unwelcome intruder. He decided against it and lumbered away. 'I'll remember this, Anderson.'

'Please do.' Her rescuer sounded indifferent, but watched until the producer had retreated down the corridor and entered the penthouse suite again. For a moment the noise of the party spilled out, then there was quiet again.

He turned to her, where she sagged against the wall, conscious of little beyond the fact that someone had come in time to save her and that she was safe. Her dress was in shreds, but she had not even the strength to cover her nakedness, only shrinking away as he came towards her.

'It's all right. He's gone.' He sounded impatient, rather than reassuring, as if he had little sympathy to waste on her—which was probably the case. She had asked for all she got. She felt his arms going round her and leaned gratefully against him, her head lolling against his broad shoulder, incapable of independent movement. For a few seconds he let her be, allowing her to recover slightly before shaking her and pushing her back against the wall. 'Come on, pull yourself together. Galveston's gone now and I haven't all night to devote to playing knight errant.'

Vanessa absorbed his words from a long way off, without really understanding them. She shook her head in an effort to clear it. 'Thank you,' she muttered thickly, as the walls spun round her giddily and then righted themselves again. 'I thought he was going to——'

The dark, rather cynical features danced before her, his mouth curving in a sardonic smile. 'He was. But you knew *that* from the start, didn't you? You encouraged him and played him on and then decided at the last minute not to go through with it. Lucky for you that I was around when you had second thoughts. Men don't like that kind of treatment, you know.'

'I'm surprised you bothered at all,' she said petulantly.

'So am I. It's a pity you didn't feel like waiting around for me. I can't say I'm flattered by your choice of substitute. Perhaps you should have been left to get what you so richly deserve for playing tricks of that sort.'

'I didn't encourage him. I——' Vanessa wanted to defend herself against the accusation, but somehow the words would not come. Belatedly aware of her state of undress, she heaved frantically at the dangling scraps of what had been her dress in an attempt to cover her bare breasts. He moved a hand towards her and she edged away from him nervously.

'Don't worry. I'm not that desperate yet, and if I was, I've no need of Sam Galveston's leavings,' he told her contemptuously. 'Anyway, I prefer my women willing. Here, take this, if you want to spare your blushes.' With a single lithe movement he stripped off his jacket and thrust it at her. Then, seeing her fumbling efforts to put it on, he swore softly under his breath and, holding her like some limp rag doll, manoeuvred her arms into the sleeves and buttoned it round her. 'Can you walk?' he demanded.

She did not think she could. Reaction was setting in fast. Her lips moved to tell him, but no sounds came out, will them though she would. It all seemed to be happening to someone else, while the real Vanessa Herbert looked on and was incapable of doing anything. If only she could wake up and find that this whole evening was just a bad dream! She tried to make her legs obey her, but they seemed to have minds of their own. All she really wanted to do was to sink to the floor and sleep.

But Max was not going to let her do anything of the sort.

'Come on, will you?' Roughly he shook her and then, supporting her wilting body, forced her tottering steps along the corridor.

'Where are we going?' she asked feebly. She seemed to recall saying those words to someone else recently. It took a tremendous effort of will to get the words out.

'To sober you up, if that's possible,' he said. 'Stay there a moment.'

He propped her up against the wall and left her. The dim whine of machinery somewhere in the background indicated to Vanessa's tired brain that there must be a lift somewhere. Where *was* he taking her? A sudden wave of panic flooded through her. How did she know that his plans for her were not running on the same lines as Sam Galveston? Just now he had told her he found her unattractive, but before that, at the party, he had made it clear that he was interested in her.

Jonathan would know what to do. He would look after her. All she had to do was to find him. Without thinking she turned and stumbled in the direction of the door leading back to the main suite.

'What the hell are you doing!' Behind her she heard Max Anderson's sharp reaction and the sound of his steps in pursuit of her. She tried to move away, but suddenly her head was full of strange music and flashing lights and the world was spinning like a merry-go-round. Where was Jonathan? Who was this grim-faced stranger who had caught hold of her again and was trying to restrain her?

'I think,' she said carefully, articulating the words as clearly as she could, although it was almost beyond her powers, 'I think I'm going to faint.'

And, as the floor came up to meet her, her last conscious thought was of the strength of Max Anderson's arms around her as he caught her to him.

CHAPTER THREE

THE hissing sound of the shower woke Vanessa the next morning. For a moment she lay there with her eyes closed, registering the sound without really thinking about it. Then, realising that if Jill was stirring it must be time to get up, she made the effort, opening her sleep-heavy eyes and wincing as she was half blinded by the strong sunlight that streamed through the window opposite the bed. That had been some party last night! She groaned and buried her head in the pillows again.

It was a few seconds before it dawned on her that in her bedroom at Jill's flat there was no window directly opposite the bed. Cautiously she dragged up one eyelid, then the other, and peered round her in bemused fashion. A quick impression of cream walls, floor-to-ceiling fitments and a rich chestnut brown carpet confirmed her first glimpse. This wasn't Jill's flat. She was in a strange bed in a bedroom that she had never seen in her life before. And, what was more, it was a double bed and the imprint of someone else's head was clearly visible on the pillow beside her.

If it wasn't Jill's flat, it wasn't Jill who was using the shower. Vanessa groaned as she sat up rather too suddenly for her present state of health. The bedclothes felt heavy and restricting against her bare skin, bringing home to her with a further shock the fact that she was as naked as the day she was born. She put a hand to her head, brushing away the strands of hair from her hot forehead, and tried to force her brain to work. A little man with a hammer was doing a tap-dance inside her head and her mouth felt horribly dry.

Where on earth was she? How had she got there? And, more important still, who owned this place? The questions chased through her mind, begging answers that refused to come. She thought back to the events of the previous evening. The party—yes, she remembered that well enough, and going there with Jonathan. Then, with a shudder, she recalled the meeting with Max Anderson and her rebound into the clutches of Sam Galveston.

It had been Max Anderson who saved her. But what had happened then? Vanessa frowned with the effort of trying to remember. She supposed she must have fainted or something. Was it Max Anderson who had brought her here afterwards? Was this his flat? And had she shared his bed? She turned cold at the thought. Presumably whoever had brought her to this place and put her to bed had been responsible for undressing her. What else had happened while she had been dead to the world?

She lay back against the pillow and considered her situation. All in all everything looked rather black. What did she do now? What had she already done that she didn't know about? The sound of running water stopped and she heard a door bang noisily and footsteps outside. For one agonised moment she thought he was going to come into the bedroom and she clutched the bedclothes to her, shielding her nakedness and dreading the inevitable meeting with the man, whoever he was. Then, mercifully for her, he went past the door and into another room. Presumably the kitchen, because she heard him moving about, then the rattle of crockery and the smell of coffee drifted along the passage to her.

Breakfast. Vanessa's stomach heaved at the thought. Trust a man to carry on as usual, as if nothing out of the ordinary had happened! But perhaps it wasn't all that unusual for him to pick up a strange girl at a party and share his bed with her. For all she knew it was his normal behaviour pattern every night of the week. But it certainly wasn't hers. He didn't know that, of course. What kind of tramp must he think her? She cringed.

At least it seemed that she had a breathing space to prepare herself to meet him. A shower would be a good idea. It might shake off the heaviness that gripped her limbs and dulled her brain at the moment. Vanessa tugged one of the sheets from the bed and pulled it towards her. She swung her legs to the floor and gasped as the room spun around her. She would be all right as soon as she made it to the bathroom, she told herself, and, wrapping the sheet firmly around her, she groped her way unsteadily to the door.

She opened it cautiously and paused, wondering if he had heard her. Then she peered into the passage outside. The bathroom was to the left, she thought. To the right a half-open door revealed kitchen cabinets and a fridge. She did not look any further, but, hitching up the sheet so that she would not trip over it, tiptoed out. Once in the bathroom, with the door safely locked, she relaxed slightly. The confrontation was only postponed, but at least she might feel more like a human being by the time she faced him.

The bathroom was still steamy from his shower and she could smell the tang of the soap that he used, a clean masculine scent that dispelled the doubt that had been hovering at the back of her mind as to the owner of all this. Sam Galveston had used a musky aftershave that had overpowered her with its sickly sweetness; this soap couldn't belong to him. She felt slightly relieved. Even if the idea of the other contender for the favour daunted her, the thought of Sam's fat little hands on her naked body repelled her.

She peered at herself in the mirror and shuddered. What a sketch she looked! Hair all over the place, her face blotchy with stale make-up and dark shadows under her eyes, the results either of smudged mascara or her heavy night, she wasn't sure which. It was going to take little short of a miracle to restore herself to something approaching normality.

She stood for some time under the shower, letting its stinging needles rouse her. There was nothing with which to shield her hair from the spray, so she gave up and doused her head too. After she had dried the rest of her on one of the large, fluffy towels that hung on a nearby rail, her hair dropped in damp black strands to her shoulders. It was too much to hope that there would be such things as hair-driers in a man's bathroom, but she opened the wall cabinet just in case. No hair-drier, but, joy of joys, something of equal value: a packet of Alka-Seltzer. Vanessa dropped two of the tablets in a glass of water, watched them fizz and drank the concoction gratefully.

She felt a little better as she donned the sheet again and made her way back to the bedroom without encountering anyone. There hadn't been a bathrobe or dressing-gown anywhere that she could purloin, so she supposed she would have to put on last night's clothes, however incongruous they looked in the light of day. Her evening dress must be in quite a state if she recalled her encounter with Sam Galveston correctly. She found its tattered remains on the bedroom floor along with her torn panty hose and her minuscule bikini briefs. One of her strappy silver sandals was retrieved from under the bed, but the other seemed to have vanished completely.

She could scarcely face the man with no clothes on,

whatever state of undress he had seen her in last night. She flinched at the thought. A glance round the room offered no solution and she hesitated to ransack his wardrobe without his permission. It would have to be the sheet again. Draping it securely round her, toga style, she braced herself and made for the kitchen. The longer she put it off, the worse the meeting would be.

Max Anderson had his back to her when she entered the room and her first sight of him was of a pair of strong, muscled bare legs topped by a brief towelling robe that, to Vanessa's eyes, was only just decent. His hair was tousled and, like hers, damp from the shower. He looked in the peak of condition, alert and active. *He* hadn't got a hangover. *He* wouldn't have, she thought bitterly.

She couldn't just stand here like a spare part, waiting for him to turn and notice her. She must take the initiative. 'Good morning,' she said with a nonchalance that she was far from feeling.

He turned and eyed her. 'So you've surfaced at last, have you? Do you want some breakfast?'

The thought of food nauseated her. 'Just some coffee would be fine, thank you.'

He raised a sardonic brow and, not noticeably sympathetic, asked, 'Head bad this morning?'

'I'm fine, thanks,' she lied. 'Just not hungry.'

'Good. We've got some talking to do.' That sounded ominous. He took the percolator, poured her a cup and pushed it across the kitchen table towards her. He didn't invite her to sit down, but she did so anyway. Standing too long, like everything else, was a strain this morning. Hot, black and strong, the coffee steamed invitingly. 'Milk? Sugar?'

She took the sugar bowl and added an unaccustomed two spoonfuls to the cup. Sugar gave one energy, didn't it? She had a feeling that she was going to need some kind of stimulus before she was much older.

'Well, I *am* hungry. You don't mind, if I carry on with——' he asked with exaggerated politeness, gesturing towards the electric hob where bacon was sizzling gently in a pan.

'Go ahead.' Vanessa hoped she would not disgrace herself by having to make a sudden dash to the bathroom. She had a shrewd suspicion that he knew exactly how she was feeling this morning and was deliberately playing up to it.

She stirred the cup vigorously and wished the banging in her head would go away. She studied Max from under her lashes. Nothing from his manner suggested that he had spent the night sleeping with a total stranger. And was sleeping all he had done? He was hardly the sort to be embarrassed, but he didn't look particularly triumphant either. For all his reputation he didn't strike her as the sort of man to take advantage of a girl without her agreement. But maybe he thought she had consented? If he hadn't, what was she doing here?

He turned the bacon out of the pan on to a plate, cut himself a hunk of bread and buttered it and brought the food to the table, eating with a heartiness that was not assumed. He ate in silence and she watched him, sipping her coffee and getting more nervous by the minute. What had happened last night? Was he going to tell her? She fidgeted, playing with her coffee spoon. How did one ask a man what he had done after one had passed out on him?

Finally he pushed the plate away and poured himself some coffee. 'Would you like some more?'

She accepted gratefully. He took a long gulp of his coffee and then studied her carefully. Exactly as if he could read what was going through her mind and was deliberately choosing to prolong the agony, he asked, 'Did you sleep well?'

'I must have done,' she said tautly. 'I don't remember.'

'No, you were pretty far gone, weren't you?' His tone was purely conversational. He could have been discussing the weather, damn him. 'But I don't suppose that's a new experience for you.'

'If you think I make a habit of behaving the way I did last night, you're very much mistaken.'

He shrugged. 'There's no need to make excuses for your actions. I'm not that interested.'

'No? You should be. It was all your fault,' Vanessa flared.

'Really? How do you work that one out? As far as I'm concerned I'm only the fool who interfered for long enough to save you from the consequences of your stupid behaviour. Perhaps you'd rather I hadn't bothered?'

She winced, knowing all too well what the outcome would have been if he hadn't chosen to interrupt at the precise moment that she needed help. 'I didn't realise he was like that until we got outside,' she defended herself. 'By then it was too late——'

He laughed unpleasantly. 'Quite the dewy innocent! Don't expect me to believe *that*. Not after the effort you put in to make such an impression on me earlier in the evening. You know when a man's interested in you. All women do.'

'It wasn't like that. You don't understand.'

'Don't I? I'm not that much of an idiot. You couldn't be bothered to wait until I came back, could you? Or did you see Sam Galveston on his own and decide that he had more to offer you? You waited until my back was turned and made a dive for him. You're not very discriminating in your choice of men. He's the worst lecher in Globe Television, and that's saying quite a lot. He must really have thought his luck was in when you threw yourself at him.'

'He said he wanted to tell me about his new series,' Vanessa persisted.

'And of course, being sweet sixteen and trusting, you believed him. Don't make me laugh!'

'So what do you think happened?' she demanded furiously.

'I think it's fairly obvious to someone with limited intelligence. Do I really have to spell it out? You were on the make. What was it you were after that you thought half an hour in a dimly lit corridor with that little creep would do the trick? Something to do with the new series? A part in it, perhaps? Sam's not that gullible, you know. I don't think the sacrifice would have produced any concrete results. At least, not the ones you were expecting.'

Her face flamed. 'Do you have to be so crude?'

'I'd say I was realistic. And I fail to see that it's my fault if you drank rather more than you could comfortably cope with in an effort to make Sam Galveston seem more palatable.'

'As far as I was concerned anyone would have been preferable to you,' she said heatedly. 'I was in a fair way to loathing you last night before I even met you, and your behaviour last night when you did introduce yourself only confirmed my opinion.'

'So I was right. You were hiding something.' He frowned. 'What am I supposed to have done to you?'

'You ruined my life, that's all—a mere detail to the mighty Max Anderson. Not worth losing any sleep over, so don't bother——'

'Don't worry, I won't,' he assured her coolly. 'Cut

the melodramatics, will you? Do I know you from somewhere? I had a feeling last night that there was something vaguely familiar about you.'

'So I strike a chord in your memory, do I? That's great!' Vanessa almost spat the words at him. 'But I suppose you meet such a host of interesting people every hour of the day. It must be hard to keep track of them all. Why should I rate a second thought in that wonder brain of yours?'

'So you've got claws, have you? I thought the sugary approach was beginning to wear a little thin last night. The irritation was showing through.' The tawny eyes gleamed with something that might have been an appreciation of the situation he had placed her in.

'I'm sorry, I don't find it funny.'

'Look——' He broke off impatiently. 'What *is* your name? I can't keep calling you nothing.'

'That didn't seem to bother you too much last night before you were called away!'

'Otherwise I might have discovered what all this was about then, instead of at this godless hour of the morning.'

'I'm Vanessa Herbert,' she told him coldly.

'I gather from your tone of voice that it's supposed to mean something to me.'

'Doesn't it?'

A well-shaped hand drummed irritably on the table top. 'I dislike guessing games. If you ever get to know me better, you'll learn to avoid them.'

'I'll bear it in mind,' she said sarcastically.

'So, you're Vanessa Herbert and I've ruined your life. We progress by leaps and bounds. Might one be permitted to ask for further details?'

'Oh, very witty! If you really want to know I'll tell you. I'm an actress. Most people thought I was quite good. And I had a job until you decided to play God and interfere.'

'Herbert. Vanessa Herbert,' he mused, then snapped his fingers. 'Of course! John Sampson's latest. Bridge, wasn't it, or some such idiocy?'

'*Pontoon*,' she corrected him prissily.

'And you've got the part of the young girl——'

'*Had* the part of the young girl, until a certain Max Anderson gave me the thumbs down. It folded a month ago. But you obviously haven't noticed that.'

'No, I can't say I had.'

'You just give your views and forget the whole thing. The casualties don't matter, do they?'

'Not much,' he said calmly, then echoed Jonathan's words to her. 'It's customary. It's the law of the jungle. You fight or you fall to the bottom of the heap.'

'That's easier said than done.'

'If you really think that, you shouldn't be doing the job in the first place,' he said cuttingly. 'Thousands of your colleagues since the year dot have been learning that lesson. What makes you so different?'

'It was my first time in the West End——'

'Well, what did you expect—instant stardom? Your name in lights, the press queue down the street to inter-view you, public acclaim?'

'I expected a fair chance.'

'And you got it, just the same as everybody else. And, if I remember rightly, you made quite a hash of it.'

'You certainly didn't throw me any bouquets,' she said bitterly.

'You didn't merit them. Why should I?' he argued, reasonably enough.

'So I'm out of a job now.'

'My heart bleeds for you. You'll just have to pick yourself up and start again.'

'I can do without the homespun philosophising, thanks,' she told him.

'Sweetness and light aren't my forte, I'm afraid.' It didn't sound like an apology and she was sure it wasn't intended to be one.

'I can tell that. You enjoy tearing people to shreds, don't you?' Vanessa accused.

He shrugged casually. 'About as much as you probably enjoy the necessary evils of your job. Selling yourself to men like Sam Galveston for promised favours must drag after a while. Or don't you find it so? At least I'm honest about my likes and dislikes.'

'How dare you?' She had to clench her hands hard around the coffee cup she was holding to stop herself throwing it at him.

'Wasn't that exactly what you were doing last night? Being dishonest?'

She sprang to her feet. 'I don't have to listen to this! I'm not staying here to be insulted——'

'Scared of listening to a few home truths about yourself?' he taunted her savagely. He thrust back his chair and got up too. The strength and power of the man intimidated her, but she stood her ground. Max Anderson wasn't going to break her this time, whatever he had done in the past!

'You're twisting everything out of all proportion,' she said.

'Am I? You claim that you hate me. But last night you were making up to me as if I was the only man in the room.' He laughed briefly. 'Perhaps you're a better actress than I gave you credit for.'

This wasn't the moment to explain what she had been attempting last night. Not that he would believe her even if she did. 'Or perhaps I wasn't acting at all,' Vanessa suggested. 'Maybe I was just bowled over by your powerful personality. Or was it your animal magnetism?'

'It's happened before now.' There was a faint, reminiscent smile on his face.

She could imagine it. He was handsome enough to disarm most women. Last night, with all the trappings of sophistication, he had looked superb. The well-cut dinner suit had moulded his powerful figure to perfection. But this morning, in a casual robe, the attraction was still there in the tilt of that firm chin, the healthy look to his skin, so different from the sickly pallor of most media personalities whom she had met, the curl in his dark hair that had been so ruthlessly repressed the previous night. At the party he had looked exactly what he was: a sleek, male animal, completely at home in the jungle he had chosen to inhabit. For all the careless air about him this morning Max Anderson was dangerous. And it would pay to remember that, Vanessa reminded herself.

It was pure folly to taunt him, but she couldn't stop herself. 'Oh, I'm sure you appeal to the baser instincts of most women.'

'And you claim to be immune, of course?'

Vanessa didn't like the way he said the words, as if he knew something that she didn't. She wished for the hundredth time that she knew more about what had happened last night. 'I didn't say that,' she fenced uneasily, and took a step backwards, away from him.

'Very wise,' he commented. 'But you would be, wouldn't you, about declaring your true feelings? I realised last night that you didn't have the courage of your convictions. You wouldn't have been struggling so hard with Sam if you'd been able to make up your mind to go through with it.'

'Really?' She tried to sound politely bored and failed

dismally. He knew how to hit out when it suited him.

'Really,' he confirmed. 'You're all talk and no action, Vanessa. You promise and then don't deliver.'

'It seems to bother you. What did I ever promise you?'

'Nothing. As yet.'

'Nor ever will, if I can help it,' she claimed vehemently.

'Don't be too sure of *that*.'

'Are you suggesting that I owe you something more for last night?'

'And if I was?'

'If you were any kind of gentleman——' began Vanessa, horribly conscious that she sounded as if she had come straight from a Victorian parsonage.

'I'm not,' he said flatly. 'I thought you'd realised that. And, as you scarcely merit being described as a lady, it shouldn't worry you too much. You haven't any finer feelings.'

'Just like you, in fact,' she blazed, throwing caution to the winds. 'We ought to be soul mates. Anyway, I'm sure your motives last night weren't that disinterested.'

'Meaning?'

'It wasn't an accident that you came and found us, was it?'

'No. I made it my business to track you down.'

'Why should you care about finding me?'

'Perhaps I like to call the tune,' he said coolly. 'I'm not accustomed to being tossed aside so casually.'

So she had scored a slight hit, after all. 'You mean you acted like a dog who'd had a choice bone stolen and wanted to get it back?'

'Possibly,' he conceded. 'Are you sorry I did?'

'No.' Vanessa looked down and found with faint surprise that she was still frantically clutching her coffee cup. She roused herself and walked over to put it in the sink. She stood with her back to him and made her next words studiedly casual. 'And afterwards?'

'After you passed out on me, you mean?'

'Yes.' She swallowed hard. 'You brought me back here.'

'There wasn't much else I could do with you. I didn't know who the hell you were. Your evening bag contained a handkerchief, a bottle of perfume and a door-key that could have fitted any one of a million doors in London,' he said impatiently. 'I'm not Sherlock Holmes. Of course I brought you back here. Would you have preferred it if I'd toted you into the party and asked if anyone could identify you? That would have caused quite a stir.'

'No, of course not. I wasn't thinking.' But he had not explained everything. She turned to face him, willing herself to remain expressionless and wondering how to go on.

But Max Anderson was a keen observer. His eyes narrowed as he looked over at her. 'Or have you been thinking too much? What's biting you?'

'Nothing.'

'Oh, yes, I think there is. You're wondering if I took my payment in full last night while you were out cold.'

'Do you blame me for wondering? You've just admitted that you're no gentleman.'

'I don't need to sink to those levels,' he said contemptuously. 'I brought you here. I undressed you—you weren't capable of doing it for yourself. As you may or may not have noticed, this is a one-bedroomed flat. I didn't see why I should crucify myself on the living-room sofa when there was a perfectly good double bed available. And you weren't raising any objections about the propriety or otherwise of my actions. Satisfied? Is that plain enough for you?'

'Yes,' she muttered, feeling an utter fool.

'But, as you seem to expect me to take advantage of you, and I'm never one to refuse an invitation when it's offered——' Before she was even aware of what he intended he had moved forward and seized her in his arms.

'What do you think you're doing?' she demanded indignantly.

'Don't ask stupid questions,' he commanded, and then, as she protested further, silenced her himself as his mouth came down on hers.

She had been kissed before, of course, but not like this. Vanessa acknowledged that truth only seconds after the touch of that hard, rather cynical mouth on hers. If he chose, Max Anderson knew exactly how to arouse a woman's senses and, with calm deliberation, that was just what he was doing to her.

At first the very suddenness of his action had stunned her into shocked immobility and she offered him no resistance. Then realisation dawned, and she struggled. But the arms that held her dealt mercilessly with her attempts to free herself and then the insistent power of his kiss drugged her and deprived her of the strength to fight him off. Against that skilled assault there was no defence, and Vanessa succumbed to the inevitable, her body crying out for more than just his kisses even while her mind was warning her that she was a fool to do so.

Waves of sensation ran through her as Max pressed her closer to him, pulling away the folds of the sheet that enveloped her and letting his fingers trace a tantalising path down her spine. She was responding eagerly now, her mouth opening under the insistence of his and giving back kiss for kiss. Her hand moved to draw aside the edges of his robe and pressed itself against the hair-roughened wall of his chest, delighting in the feel of him. She gave herself up totally to the

pleasure of his touch, caring only that this could go on
for ever.

She came back to the world of sanity with a sudden
shock when he released her abruptly to ask, 'Shall we
go back to bed?'

The words fell like stones on her conscious mind.
From somewhere she found the strength to thrust him
from her and stumble aside.

'I take it that means the answer's no.'

She looked at him, hating him. Her head was still
reeling from shock, her body still registering its own
protest at being deprived of his lovemaking. But Max
Anderson hadn't lost his cool. He stood there, hands on
his hips, surveying her with a faintly quizzical look that
gave no hint that he was in any danger of giving way to
his emotions. She might have been turning down the
offer of another cup of coffee for all the impact her
refusal of him seemed to have on his ego.

'I want to go home,' Vanessa said. She knew she
could not take much more. The sooner she removed
herself from this man's company the better for her
peace of mind.

He didn't argue the point. 'All right. I'd better find
you something to wear. That sheet isn't a very adequate
cover.'

Hastily she swathed herself in it again, suddenly
aware of how far his roving hands had strayed.

'Don't worry, I wasn't going to try to change your
mind for you.' He sounded jaded, suddenly bored with
her. 'If you'll trust me as far as the bedroom, I think
there's a pair of jeans and a T-shirt that will do for you.
They'll be yards too big, but it doesn't matter.'

In silence she followed him and watched while he
sorted out some clothes from one of the cupboards
there. He tossed them over to her, commanding, 'Put

these on.' Then, as she hesitated, 'For heaven's sake, forget your precious chastity for a minute! Is sex all you can think about? I saw all you had to offer last night and it didn't attract me.'

But he hadn't been averse to taking advantage of her this morning, Vanessa thought. His hand went to the tie of his robe and she realised that he certainly wasn't going to consider any feelings of modesty that she might be expected to possess. He would only laugh if she protested or took herself off to the bathroom. Her eyes lingered on the muscled perfection of his body before she dragged her gaze away, scared that he would notice and comment on the fact.

She wasted little time getting dressed. As he had predicted, the jeans slid on to her hips, the legs impossibly long, and the T-shirt was baggy to say the least. But both garments, when adjusted, were a great improvement on the sheet they replaced.

'Ready?' In a black cashmere sweater and dark slacks he still retained that quality of controlled power that intimidated her.

'Yes, I suppose so.'

'I'll drive you home.'

'There's no need,' she protested. 'If you'll lend me the money for a taxi——'

'Don't be a bloody fool,' he said, and that seemed to settle the matter.

Vanessa rolled up the wreck that had been her evening dress into a tight bundle along with her solitary shoe and the evening bag that she had retrieved from the bedside table where he had dropped it. Better to remove all traces of her offending presence, she thought, stuffing them under her arm. Then she followed him to the door.

A glossy black Maserati was parked at the kerb outside the flats and he unlocked the passenger door and motioned her inside without a word, before taking his own seat. 'Where are we heading for?' he asked her.

She gave Jill's address and began to offer directions. 'It's all right, I know it,' he said, cutting her short.

To judge by the speed he drove at, he obviously wanted to be rid of her as soon as was humanly possible. Vanessa glanced at the hard, unsmiling profile and wondered what he was thinking. Probably blaming her for wasting his time, both last night and this morning. Max Anderson was not accustomed to unscheduled disturbances in his smooth-running life and a girl who brought him nothing but inconvenience could hardly expect the red carpet treatment that he no doubt dished out to some people. It was strange that he had even bothered to drive her home. She sank back in her seat, devoutly hoping that the journey would be a short one.

For the first time it occurred to her that Jill must be worried sick about her. What had her sister thought when she had not come home from the party? She had never stayed out all night before. She wasn't the type. Would Jonathan have rung to ask what had happened to her? And what must *he* be thinking? Vanessa grew more anxious by the second.

Max Anderson must have noticed her preoccupied air. 'Having regrets?' he taunted her.

What did he mean? Regrets that she hadn't gone to bed with him? That was what he would think, of course. Any girl who turned down the chance would inevitably have second thoughts. The nerve of the man! She had no intention of being drawn on the subject. 'Only that I was ever unlucky enough ever to have met you,' she snapped at him.

He laughed harshly. 'The feeling's mutual, believe me.'

He turned his attention back to the road, frowning slightly, and they completed the rest of the journey in a strained silence that did nothing for Vanessa's tautly stretched nerves. With relief she saw the familiar Hampstead landmarks come into view and roused herself to direct him to the large Victorian house, the basement of which was Jill's flat, situated in one of the roads near the southern end of the Heath. There didn't seem to be any panda cars parked outside, so perhaps Jill hadn't got as far as having the river dragged yet.

Vanessa gathered up her things and had the door open almost before the car had come to a halt in her haste to get away. She didn't care what Max Anderson thought about her any more. She just wanted to get as great a distance as possible from him and subside into a hearty bout of tears.

'Thank you for the lift,' she said over her shoulder as she exited faster than she had ever left a car in her life. Then she slammed the door behind her and took to her heels, running for sanctuary as if from the devil himself.

CHAPTER FOUR

ONCE safely inside, with the reassurance of a sturdy front door between herself and the man she had just left, Vanessa stood for a moment in the tiny hall, panting with effort and trying desperately to listen for sounds that would indicate that Max Anderson had taken exception to her rush away from him and had come in pursuit. The bolt that she had slammed home looked strong enough, but she didn't hold out much hope of it surviving a determined attack from Max Anderson. He wasn't the sort of man to let a little thing like that get in his way. She shivered slightly. Then, with relief, she heard the harsh crash of gears as the Maserati turned and the rev of its engine as he speeded away. He was not wasting any more time on her. But, by the sound of it, he was angry. Well, so was she. And Max Anderson didn't have to face a sister who was probably demented with worry by now. She braced herself and headed for the living room.

'Jill? Are you there?'

Silence. And no one in the kitchen, either. Vanessa flung open the door of Jill's bedroom to see it in its usual pristine condition, the bed made and everything in its place. A further check revealed that her sister's coat and handbag had gone. Thoroughly alarmed by now, she tried her own room, where a note slipped under the door solved the mystery.

'Waited up till 2 a.m. for you, then gave it up. I'm a working girl, remember? I suppose you crawled in at dawn. Hope you had a good time. Bacon in frying pan, if you feel like any breakfast. Tell me all about it tonight. Love, Jill.'

Why was everyone so keen to force food on her this morning? Vanessa screwed the paper into a small ball and threw it viciously into the corner of the room. So Jill hadn't even missed her. She had gone to work as usual, not suspecting that anything was wrong. At least that was one less set of explanations to make. She sighed. Her brain still felt like cotton wool. More coffee would be a good idea. The two cups that she had downed already today hadn't gone even halfway to making her feel human again.

She sat down on the living room sofa and cradled a steaming mug of coffee in her hands as she reviewed the situation. The next person to be dealt with was Jonathan. Vanessa eyed the phone dismally. One didn't treat Jonathan the way that she had done last night, disappearing without any explanation and leaving him to hunt high and low for her when he decided it was time to leave. What must he have thought? Better to get explanations over with, she thought, and reached for the receiver.

Jonathan wasn't at home, but her second call to his office found him. 'You got home all right, then?' he asked. 'I was just about to ring you.' Amazingly, he didn't sound either offended or cross. If anything he was faintly placatory.

She paused, her words of apology dying on her lips. 'Yes, thank you,' she said cautiously, still testing the ground.

'Good!' The heartiness in Jonathan's voice was a little overdone. 'I was sure you'd manage on your own.'

'What happened to you?' Vanessa asked.

'The fact is, I met up with one of the guys from New York, and we got chatting about what's new on Broadway.'

'And?'

'In the end we decided to get away from that crush and find a quiet bar somewhere to talk without interruptions. He's put a lot of business my way in the past, so I didn't want to offend him.'

'No, of course not,' she said automatically. She felt an insane desire to laugh. The boot was on the other foot with a vengeance!

'You're not annoyed with me, Vanessa love? I did look for you, but you seemed to have vanished.'

That was probably when she was playing catch-as-catch-can with Sam Galveston. 'No, I'm not annoyed.' Relief made her tone as hearty as his.

'You found someone to amuse yourself with?'

'You could put it like that,' she said dryly.

'I was worried about you,' he insisted. 'I should have seen you home.'

'No need, I managed myself,' she assured him. With a little help from Max Anderson, but she wasn't going to tell Jonathan about *that*.

After a few more protestations Jonathan allowed himself to be convinced that he had acted perfectly reasonably in abandoning her to her fate and rang off, satisfied.

So much for supposing that her nearest and dearest had been remotely concerned about her, Vanessa thought ruefully. But thank goodness that things had turned out the way they had. Jonathan was in a good humour because she hadn't made a fuss, and Jill was none the wiser. She wondered how much of last night's episode to reveal to her sister. Definitely an edited version. She had no intention of parading her bruised emotions in front of anyone, however sympathetic.

In that case it might be better to get rid of the evidence. She glanced down at her clothes and pulled a face, then went to her room to change. As she tugged the borrowed T-shirt over her head she caught a faint impression of the body cologne that Max used and had a sudden vivid memory of its clean tanginess on his skin when he had drawn her close to him and kissed her. But that was best forgotten, she told herself firmly as she packed his clothes up.

There was no need for a covering note. He would know who had sent them. Unless, of course, he made a habit of kitting out stray females. But Vanessa was willing to bet that most of the women who shared his bed came better prepared than she had done. She found his address in the telephone book, printed it on the parcel and set out for the Post Office, although she felt more like collapsing in a heap on her bed. She did just that when the vital errand was done and, after a few hours' badly needed sleep, revived enough to face the thought of getting herself a snack and set about making the evening meal ready for Jill's return.

'Well, how did it go?' Her sister was barely through the door that night before she asked the question.

Vanessa managed to sound fairly convincing. 'Fine— I enjoyed it. I'm glad you nagged me to go. Come and eat and I'll bore you with all the details.'

'Fat chance,' Jill laughed. 'I'm a sucker for hearing about the high life. It's nice to hobnob with the famous, even by proxy.'

She listened avidly as Vanessa reeled off the names of those who had been there. 'You were mixing with the notables, love. Anyone else I'm likely to have heard of?'

Vanessa took a deep breath. 'Oh, yes.' She tried to sound casual. 'Max Anderson was there.'

'The ogre in person? Did he recognise you?'

'No,' she said briefly.

'So you didn't get a chance to meet him?'

She dodged the issue, unwilling to tell a downright

lie. 'He was holding court surrounded by hordes of people.'

'Oh.' Jill sounded dashed.

'Did you think he'd make a beeline for me and apologise? It doesn't happen except in fairy tales.'

'No, you idiot. But I did have a horrid feeling that you might get in a rage with him if you were unlucky enough to meet up. I know you and your temper of old. It's probably just as well you weren't given the chance of talking to him.'

'Mm,' Vanessa said non-committally. 'Don't worry, I recognise superior strength when I see it. Trying to throw him would be like trying to overturn a ten-ton truck with a matchstick. Hey, did I tell you your favourite TV detective was there?' Adroitly she changed the subject and was thankful when her sister followed her lead quite happily.

If only she could dismiss the man from her thoughts as easily as she had turned the conversation away from him. As she lay tossing about in bed that night, strangely incapable of sleep, Max Anderson's dark, expressive features haunted her. Vanessa replayed the entire encounter. Why hadn't she managed it better? What kind of idiot was she? She cursed herself for the opportunities she had missed, for the woeful inadequacies of her responses to his remarks.

Never in her life had she hated anyone quite so much as she hated him. And yet she had tamely submitted to his kisses with only a token show of resistance. What was it about the man that had turned her initial struggles to a state of pliant desire? Chemical attraction, pure and simple, she decided. Emotions had nothing to do with it, rational thoughts even less. The problem nagged at her brain for a long time before she finally slept.

She woke next morning sure of one thing at least: she was going to make a new beginning. Jill and Jonathan were right and she had been wrong. No more skulking about the flat as if she had something to hide. It was time to get out and prove that Max Anderson was wrong about her acting ability. If a little voice at the back of her mind suggested that his advice to her had been along more or less the same lines, she ignored it.

'It's about time I pulled my weight with the house-keeping,' she told Jill briskly over breakfast. 'I've sponged off you for far too long.'

'Rubbish! What are families for?' But Vanessa could tell that her sister was pleased by the news.

A call to Jonathan to ask if there were any acting jobs in the offing that she could try for drew a blank. But she wasn't too discouraged. From now on optimism must be the keynote.

'You'll let me know if anything turns up that might suit me?' she asked Jonathan with something approaching her old enthusiasm.

'Sure. I'm glad to know that you've come to your senses at last,' he told her. 'I'll be in touch.'

'No luck?' Jill queried.

'No, but I'm not expecting miracles. I'll find something as a fill-in,' Vanessa announced. 'Thank goodness you made me take that dreary secretarial course when I was still at drama school.'

'I told you it would come in useful some day.'

'And so it has. I'll come out with you this morning and see about getting some temporary work.' She sounded a good deal more confident than she felt. After all, it must be four years or more since she had touched a typewriter.

But her luck was in. After a few false starts her old skills came back remarkably quickly and the girl at the agency she visited viewed the results of her typing test with approval.

'We'll have no trouble placing you,' she said. 'When do you want to start?'

'As soon as possible. I need the money,' Vanessa admitted.

'There's a solicitor in Hounslow who wants some copy typing done,' the other girl offered. 'It'll be deadly dull, but if you'd like to try it——'

'I'll take it.' She couldn't afford to be choosy.

It was the first of any number of jobs, some boring, some fascinating, that Vanessa took on during the next month. She worked for chartered accountants, doctors, financiers and advertising men. Her employers ranged from whizz-kids with long hair and floral shirts to sober-suited city businessmen. On the whole she enjoyed herself and the money that she brought home was very welcome, but the thought of typing every day for the rest of her working life appalled her.

'I don't know how you stand it,' she said to Jill. 'At least I move around and get a change of scene. You're stuck in the same office with the same people day after day. Don't you ever feel like slaughtering them?'

'Frequently.' Her sister laughed. 'But fortunately the impulse passes. I'm not like you, Van. I just want a quiet life.'

'Mine's certainly that at the moment,' Vanessa complained. 'Only three auditions in the last fortnight and nothing came of any of them. Sometimes I think Jonathan isn't trying hard enough.'

'Give him time. There'll be something soon.'

'That's what he says.' Vanessa sighed. 'Meanwhile, back to slaving over a hot typewriter.'

The girl at the agency was a friend by now and she greeted Vanessa with a bright smile the next day. 'I've got something in this morning that will suit you down to the ground.'

'No typing and lots of money?' Vanessa hazarded with a grin. 'Don't tell me my luck's in at last.'

'Hardly that. But half the girls on our books would dive at the chance to take this one on. Just to meet him would be a treat, let alone work for him.'

'Sounds like fun.' Vanessa leaned against the desk and inspected a scuffed shoe, before going on. 'Well, tell me more about this wonder. Is it Robert Redford?'

'Not quite that league. But *I* think he's much more attractive.' The other girl looked dreamy. 'Last time he was on the box I couldn't take my eyes off him. I always prefer dark men, don't you? And those eyes of his—they sort of hold you. You know what I mean?'

The faintest of suspicions crossed Vanessa's mind and was then firmly banished. *He* wasn't the only dark-haired man who appeared on television. Pull yourself together, girl. It was probably some long-haired pop star she had never heard of.

'I was bored stiff with Shakespeare and all that stuff when I did it at school, but somehow he makes it interesting. Of course he's got a lovely voice. He could make a fortune doing commercials. I'd buy anything he told me to.'

'Who?' asked Vanessa patiently.

'Max Anderson, of course. Who do you think?'

The words were a jolt, even though, subconsciously, she had somehow been expecting them. She had made a determined effort to forget the man and their disastrous meeting in the last month and she thought she had managed it. The violence of her reaction now only showed her how unsuccessful she had been.

'Are you all right? You've gone as white as a sheet.'

Vanessa heard the words from a distance, then pulled herself together and tried to answer convincingly. 'Yes,

I'm fine really. I slept in this morning and came out without any breakfast. Stupid of me. It must be just hitting me.'

'Shall I get you some coffee?'

'What? Oh, no, thanks, I'll be fine in a minute.'

'You'd better not do that sort of thing when you're working for Max Anderson,' the girl advised her. 'He may look gorgeous, but he's all there, you can tell that, and he doesn't strike me as the sympathetic type.'

You can say that again! thought Vanessa. In a sort of haze she heard the agency girl giving her the details of the assignment.

'Look, I've written down the address. It's not that far from where you live, is it? Only a bus ride. He wants someone to go round this morning at eleven o'clock. I said it would be O.K. Vanessa?'

She roused herself. 'Yes?'

'You do want it, don't you?' The other girl sounded faintly aggrieved. 'You know, I saved it specially for you, you being in the same line of business, as it were.'

'Thank you,' Vanessa managed. 'That was kind of you. But I don't think——'

'He's offering double the usual money if you meet his deadline. It's something he wants done in a hurry and his usual girl let him down, apparently.'

'Yes, I see. But——'

'I should step on it, if I were you. It's nearly ten now and you know what the buses are like at this time of day.'

Vanessa hesitated. It was clearly impossible to duck the situation by merely saying she didn't want to work for the man without giving some adequate explanation. The last thing she wanted was for the agency to think that she was difficult to place. And if she said that she was ill, there would be no other work forthcoming.

Then a flash of the temper about which Jill was

always warning her made up her mind for her. Darn the man! She wasn't turning down good money just for the sake of avoiding him. She would take the job. If anyone was going to back out, let it be him. She couldn't imagine he would be all that delighted by the agency's choice of secretary for him.

'I'll be off, then.' She picked up her bag and said a quick goodbye, eager to get on her way before doubts set in as to the wisdom of her actions. She found the apartment block in St John's Wood without much trouble and entered it confidently, but by the time she emerged from the lift on to the small landing outside his top floor flat, her heart was thumping unevenly and her palms were sticky with apprehension. A sort of bravado carried her to the door and enabled her to ring the bell. It took all her strength to stand there and wait when all she wanted to do was run away before he had a chance to answer.

'What the hell are you doing here?'

His greeting could hardly have been called encouraging. It should have withered her, but, unaccountably, it had just the opposite effect. Vanessa's chin tilted defiantly. 'The agency sent me. I'm your temporary typist.'

'You're my *what*?'

Silently she thrust the piece of paper at him with the agency's authorisation on it. He gave a thunderous frown. 'We'll see about *that*,' he said ominously. 'You'd better come in, I suppose, for the moment. We can't discuss this on the doorstep.'

He stood aside and let her precede him into the entrance hall. It was all too familiar to her. After one brief, unhappy visit the details of the place seemed engraved on her memory, even to the pictures on the walls. 'The living room's to your right.' His voice sounded just behind her and she jumped slightly with

nerves. Did he really think she would head for the bedroom?

She pushed open the door in front of her and walked
into a large, sunny room that bore ample evidence of its
owner's profession. Most of the wall-space was given
over to shelves, loaded with books on all topics, but
with the arts well represented. At one end of the room
was expensive-looking hi-fi equipment with all the latest
recording devices including a video machine. At the
other, by a large window which gave an excellent view
out over the distant green spaces of Hampstead and
beyond, was an enormous desk, its surface littered
with papers that almost obscured the typewriter placed
squarely in its centre. An old-fashioned button-backed
sofa offered the only choice of seat besides a hard office
chair, and Vanessa headed for it and sat down with an
assurance that she was certainly not feeling.

'Do make yourself at home, won't you?'

Sarcastic beast, she thought, but didn't let herself
betray any irritation. 'Thank you.' She smiled pleasantly at him instead.

'You've got a nerve coming here,' he commented.

Vanessa shrugged with assumed indifference. 'It's a
job. Out-of-work actresses can't afford to be fussy.

'But *I* can.' He turned and picked up the phone,
dialling the number with a swift, controlled precision
that told her that his anger simmered very near to the
surface. 'Hello. Is that the Keyboard agency? Anderson
here. Look, I want you to send another girl up here. I
don't like the look of this one.'

He was being deliberately offensive, she knew.
Vanessa wondered if the girl at the agency would still
go dreamy-eyed over Max Anderson after this. Probably. The famous were allowed more leeway in the
matter of good manners, it seemed, and there was no

doubt that a good-looking celebrity could get away with murder in that line. And the man at her side was not exactly ugly.

He was built more like a professional athlete than a man of letters, she thought, studying him unobserved as he argued over the phone. He was wearing a cream sweater, its sleeves rolled up to reveal strong forearms with a sprinkling of dark hair, and it did little to conceal the power of his broad shoulders and chest. The casual jeans that he had on clung with fashionable tightness and emphasised the muscled length of his legs. Her gaze roved the hard planes of his face. That firm chin saved him from the prettiness that often accompanied good looks. Firm? Obstinate rather, stubborn as a mule, absolutely determined to get his own way come hell or high water.

But for once he did not seem to be getting very far, to judge from the increasingly furious tone of his side of the conversation. A minute or two later he growled 'Goodbye' and slammed the receiver down so hard that it rocked on its cradle. He glowered at Vanessa. 'It seems I'm stuck with you.'

'I'm sorry to hear that.'

'They can't or won't send someone else. I suppose they haven't got anyone to send. They must have been scraping the bottom of the barrel with you.'

'You needn't suppose I was particularly overjoyed at the prospect of working for you,' she snapped, and got to her feet. 'I'll be quite glad to go elsewhere. There are plenty of other agencies, if you care to try them.'

'I don't. I'm not going through the whole rigmarole again. You'll have to do, although heaven only knows what kind of mess you'll make of it. Can you even type?' He sounded sceptical.

'Of course I can!'

'Well, that's a start, I suppose. Sit down, will you? I

can't bear people hovering around the place as if they're apologising for their existence.'

'Don't worry, I'm not likely to do that,' she assured him.

'No. Meek and mild you're not,' he agreed.

'Are those essential qualities in your secretarial staff? If they are, I'd better go.'

'Sit down,' he commanded, and Vanessa complied so hastily, reacting to the edge in his voice, that a faint smile crossed his face 'I'll tell you exactly what I require. He ticked off the points with one long, tapering finger. 'First and foremost, accurate, speedy typing. Then, a fair degree of common sense, a certain amount of initiative when the occasion calls for it, a pleasant voice on the phone and an ability to keep calm however many times I may lose my temper in the course of a working day.'

'Not a great deal, in fact. Anything else?' she asked him tartly.

He shot her a wicked glance, a sudden glint of devilry in his eyes. 'Good legs,' he said.

She refused to be provoked. 'And do you think that I'll be able to satisfy any of your requirements?'

'Certainly the last.' His tawny gaze lingered appreciatively over her and she resisted the impulse to tug at her skirt, which had ridden up over her knees. So much for wearing old clothes to economise! The fashions of two years ago were a little short for today's standards.

'And the rest?'

'We'll work on that as we go along,' he said calmly. 'I imagine I'll be able to lick you into some kind of shape before I've finished with you.'

She didn't like the sound of that. 'So I'm to consider myself employed, am I?'

'For a trial run,' he agreed. 'But you'll be out on your ear the first time you make a mistake.'

'I shouldn't be too critical if I were you,' she told him sweetly.

'Meaning I ought to make allowances for your inexperience, I suppose?'

'Meaning good secretaries are harder to find than you seem to think,' she corrected him.

'We have yet to establish your excellence. I'm warning you, Vanessa, that I don't suffer fools gladly.'

'There's no need. You've already made me quite aware of that. It's painfully obvious, I'm afraid.'

'Were you referring to my professional opinion of your lack of talent?' he enquired. 'Or was it something I said to you at the party? That was careless of me. I don't usually let my women know what I'm thinking about them.'

'No, that would never do. It might give the game away.' Vanessa seethed. 'But I'm not one of your women. I turned you down, if you remember.'

'Was that why you asked them to send you here? Were you looking for a second chance?'

'I'm not interested in you. Not now, not ever. Is that clear enough for you, Mr Anderson?'

'As crystal. If you mean it. And you'd better make it Max.'

'I thought that was reserved for your friends.'

'Play your cards right and I might number you among them one of these days.'

'There's a thought.' She laughed harshly. 'That's a pleasure I can forgo, thank you all the same.'

'Oh, I don't know about that. I think you could be persuaded to change your tune. What does it take to sway you, Vanessa Herbert? Money? Influence? The promise of a good part in a new play? Or something else?' His eyes were on her lips and she knew exactly what was the something else that he had in mind.

'I wouldn't advise you to try,' she said as coolly as she was able. 'You'd be wasting your valuable time.'

'That's my business, surely? But I very much doubt it.'

'Do you always get your own way?'

'Only ninety per cent of the time. The rest I put down to experience.'

'It's all a game to you, isn't it?' Vanessa accused him. 'And you're not a good loser.'

He shrugged. 'Is anyone? Are you suggesting that I've lost where you're concerned?'

'Haven't you?' she challenged. 'It looks very much like it to me. I think I'm pretty well immune to your fatal charms.'

'Do you?' He smiled, an easy, confident smile that held all the assurance in the world. 'Come on, Vanessa, we both know that's not true.'

He was reminding her of that awful morning that she had tried so hard to forget. That morning when she had gone into his arms as if it had been the most natural thing in the world. Vanessa tossed her head. 'You didn't get what you wanted that time.'

'Perhaps I wasn't trying too hard. I think that little scene would have had a different ending if I had.'

'No,' she said, as much to herself as to him. She didn't trust him an inch. He was playing with her like a cat with a captive mouse. She felt suddenly breathless. It was exciting, this verbal sparring, exhilarating even, but it was dangerous. 'Shall we get on? If you tell me what you want me to do, perhaps we can get started?'

A mobile brow registered faint mockery at her attempt to sound businesslike, and for an instant, she wondered if he would deliberately choose to put another meaning to her words. She tensed expectantly.

But she was mistaken. He motioned her to the desk. 'Did the agency pass on any details?' He went on before she had a chance to reply. 'I expect you've forgotten them already if they did.'

'They said it was something urgent and you were prepared to pay over the odds to get it done.'

'Oh, that went home at least,' he said insultingly. He rooted about impatiently amongst the mass of papers on the desk top, then produced a bundle of handwritten sheets roughly clipped together 'This is it.' He thrust it at her. 'Well?'

'Can I cope, do you mean?' Vanessa glanced at the top sheet. 'The writing's appalling, but I've had worse to decipher and managed.'

'You'll have to leave me a note if you get into difficulties with it. Or, in an emergency, I'll let you know where you'll be able to find me. But I'm a busy man, don't bother me with details.'

She looked at it again. 'It's a script of some kind.'

'Brilliantly deduced,' he said with heavy sarcasm. 'But of course, an actress would recognise that. Yes, it's a television play.'

'Yours?' she asked curiously.

'Yes.'

He wasn't exactly volunteering a wealth of information. 'I didn't know you wrote that sort of thing.'

'I haven't until now. It's my first attempt. And it's to be kept strictly confidential, if you know the meaning of the word.'

'Of course I do.'

'If that's true, you'll be the first actress who ever did,' he said caustically. He glanced at the heavy gold watch on his wrist. 'I must be going. I've an appointment in town in half an hour. Any questions?'

'No, I don't think so.'

'Your hours are nine to five unless I tell you otherwise. Sometimes I'll be here, sometimes I won't. Just carry on as usual. O.K.?'

'Yes.' She hoped he wouldn't be at home that often. It was a very small flat and she could do without his disturbing presence to upset her balance.

'I don't want you wasting time by going out for lunch,' he went on. 'Raid the fridge. There's plenty of food there and I'll see that it's kept stocked up for you.'

'Thank you.'

'If the phone rings take messages and leave them where I can find them. All you need in the way of paper and that sort of thing is in the desk drawer. I want two carbons. You know the format to use, I suppose?'

'I'm not a complete idiot!' she flared. He was talking to her as if she was a not very bright six-year-old.

'Prove it, then,' he said. 'I always did prefer deeds to words.' He stooped to pick up a dark leather jacket that was tossed carelessly on the floor and shrugged himself into it. He turned to go and Vanessa drew a breath of relief. 'Oh, and there's one more thing, Vanessa——'

'Yes?' she said with exaggerated patience.

'Don't start getting any ideas, will you?'

'What about?' She was genuinely puzzled.

He gestured towards the script in her hand. 'My play. I wouldn't want you to cherish any false hopes that there's a part in it for you. I'll be specifying good actresses for the leading roles when it's produced.'

'If it ever comes to that,' she retorted. 'What's the acceptance rate for television plays these days—one in a thousand?'

'Something like that.' He didn't sound too worried about it. 'I hope you enjoy reading it.'

'I doubt that very much,' she said rudely.

He laughed, not noticeably put out by her remark. 'You could be in for a surprise,' he said. Then the door banged behind him and he was gone.

CHAPTER FIVE

HE was right, of course; Vanessa might have known that. She did enjoy reading his play, a wicked send-up of bureaucracy which nevertheless held a few serious social comments. And, strangely enough, as the days went by, she became aware of another startling fact. She enjoyed working for Max Anderson.

Not that he was an easygoing boss by any means— far from it. He expected hard work and plenty of it and was quick to notice any drop in standards. Sloppiness and untidiness irritated him. If something did not meet with his approval it was waiting, heavily scored through, for Vanessa to retype the next day. It became almost a challenge to see how much of her work could pass muster first time round, and she was pleased with herself as she registered the improvement that came about.

'Not that *he'll* ever praise me,' she told Jill, almost bitterly. 'I could be a machine for all the notice that he takes of me.'

'Does it matter? I thought you hated the man. When you told me you were going to work for him I didn't think you'd last a week without sticking a knife into him.'

'Don't worry, I'm still tempted to do just that. Working for him hasn't changed a thing,' Vanessa assured her. 'Except that there's a certain poetic justice about the man who put me out of work having to employ me himself.'

'Did you think it might alter things?' Jill was curious.

'Was that why you took the job in the first place?'

'You mean, was I hoping to convince him that he was wrong about me?' She laughed in genuine amusement. 'What did you have in mind—a few quick passages from Shakespeare delivered in between punching the typewriter keys to make him realise that I'm really talented?'

'Of course not, idiot! But there are other ways of going about it.'

'Spread a little sweetness and light and see the man weaken at the knees?' Vanessa jeered. 'If only you knew him!'

'He's supposed to like women.'

'And they like him. But that doesn't mean that they get anywhere with him. He changes them to fit the mood of the moment. One day it's a bubbly blonde, the next a redhead. When he gets bored he moves on—and believe me, Max gets bored very quickly.'

'Don't they mind?' asked Jill.

'Sometimes.' Vanessa recalled a couple of fairly agonised messages that she'd had to relay to him. He hadn't seemed particularly disturbed by them. 'But that's their hard luck. If that man's got any finer feelings, he keeps them pretty well buried.'

'It sounds as if you're pretty well out of it, Van.'

She recognised the slightly cautionary note in her sister's voice and grinned. Jill didn't know that she'd got her fingers burnt already where Max Anderson was concerned and didn't need warning off. 'Are you scared I'll succumb to the man's devastating charms? I'd rather go ten rounds with a man-eating tiger than try my luck with him! I'm safe enough. I just feel sorry for anyone who doesn't have the sense to steer clear.'

Vanessa said as much to Max himself the next day. It was one of the rare occasions when he was at home, sprawled across the living room sofa, working at a sheaf of papers spread across his knees. Usually he left her pretty much to herself, as often as not communicating with her by phone or note from one day to the next. Vanessa preferred it that way. For all her vaunted immunity to the man she felt distinctly uneasy in his presence. When he was there the flat seemed even smaller somehow, dwarfed by his powerful build. She found it difficult to settle to her work with him in the same room and spoiled sheet after sheet of paper, ripping them furiously out of the typewriter.

He noticed. Not much passed him by. 'I hope we're well supplied with typing paper,' he commented. 'We'd need to be at the rate that you're getting through it.'

'Are you planning to dock my wages to compensate for it?' She was cross with herself for letting the fact that he was there get to her and cross with him for seeing it.

'Touchy, aren't you?' he observed.

'I don't like to feel someone breathing down my neck when I work. It puts me off.'

'I'd have thought that in your profession you'd have got used to an audience,' he said, mildly enough. 'But I agree that this flat's too small for two, unless they're on pretty intimate terms.'

'Which we're certainly not.'

'Quite.'

'You'll have to find something larger when you get married.' She didn't know what made her say that. Perhaps, by talking to him, she was trying to ease the tension she felt building up inside her every time they met.

'If I get married,' he corrected her. 'It certainly doesn't feature in my plans at the moment, whatever the gossip writers may be saying to the contrary.'

'They say you're playing the field.'

'They're right for once.' He smiled thinly. 'There's safety in numbers.'

'Scared?' she challenged.

'Should I be?'

Vanessa shrugged her shoulders casually. 'There seem to be any amount of stupid women lining up to try and catch you. If the law of averages operates one of them is bound to drag you up the aisle some day.'

'I doubt it,' he said calmly. 'I don't like stupid women.'

'I can't say that I've noticed. Those who try endlessly to get you on the phone don't seem too bright to me. It's a shame they can't take the brush-off when it comes.'

'You'd have got the message instantly and understood it, of course,' Max drawled.

'Oh, they've got the message, loud and clear. They could hardly fail to when you're seen out on the town with someone new. They just refuse to accept it.'

'Is that my fault?' he asked carelessly.

'No, it's theirs, the poor fools.'

'Then why waste any sympathy on them? They ask for all they get.'

'You despise women, don't you?' she said.

'I wouldn't say that.'

'All right, put it another way. You use them.'

'They allow themselves to be used. I'm not to blame if they get hurt in the process.'

'You never get hurt yourself, of course.'

A shuttered look came to his face and, for a second, Vanessa wondered if she had hit some hidden nerve. 'Emotion is a waste of time,' Max said harshly. 'I learnt that lesson long ago.'

'If you really think that, I'm sorry for you,' she said.

'There's no need. I concentrate quite successfully on the other areas of life.'

'Mere physical relationships don't bring lasting

happiness,' Vanessa claimed, sounding priggish even to her own ears.

'I never said they did.' He laughed. 'You would know about all that, wouldn't you?' he added with faint contempt. 'It's a case of the pot calling the kettle black. I don't think your encounter with Sam Galveston had much of the spiritual plane about it. But you didn't expect it to, did you?'

'That's none of your business!'

'No. And I'd remind you that my affairs aren't your concern either. Perhaps you'll keep your thoughts to yourself in future.'

'I'll be delighted to.' Vanessa turned back to the desk, seized some paper and fed it into the typewriter with a purposeful clatter. 'Don't worry, I know my place.'

'That I very much doubt, but I'll live in hope,' he said sourly.

She resisted the impulse to answer back and bent to her work again. This time she tried hard to get absorbed in what she was doing and, with effort, managed to forget his offending presence behind her.

'Coffee?'

She started nervously at the sound of his voice. 'What? Oh, yes, thanks.'

He disappeared to the kitchen for a few minutes and returned bearing two mugs. 'Black with two sugars, isn't it? Did I get it right?'

That was the way she had drunk it on the only other occasion that he had made coffee for her. She shifted edgily in her chair at the memory. 'I don't usually bother with sugar, but this will do,' she said ungraciously, as she accepted it.

'Dieting?' She could feel his eyes assessing her body. 'You've no need. You've got a figure that most women would envy.'

'Thank you. You would know, wouldn't you?'

'Of course.' He smiled as if recalling something pleasant.

Her face flamed with anger. 'There's no need to throw *that* at me at every opportunity!'

'The fact that I'm a connoisseur of the female form?' he asked blandly.

'The fact that you've seen more of my figure than other men have.'

'I can't believe that. Such modesty, Vanessa! Or is it that you prefer to undress in the dark?'

He was enjoying baiting her, she could tell. She felt the spark of temper inside her fan into a full-scale blaze. 'Shut up!' she snapped. 'I don't want to hear any more.'

'No? But I find it interesting.'

'I'm glad you think so. *I* don't, particularly.'

'No, it's not so pleasant, is it, when *your* private life is the one under discussion?'

'Discussion? Dissection is the word!'

He ignored the protest. 'Tell me, how many men have there been, Vanessa? Or have you lost count?' he asked pleasantly.

Without conscious thought she raised the mug and threw its contents squarely at him. He dodged and the hot liquid just missed his face, spreading instead in a dark stain down his sweater and trousers. Vanessa stood aghast, her hand going to her mouth in horror.

'You little vixen!' The fury in his voice broke the spell that held her rooted to the spot and, in a blind panic to escape him, she ran for the door. She didn't know where she was going, just anywhere away from the icy rage that she saw in his face. 'Oh, no, you don't!' Strong arms halted her long before she reached her target and pulled her back towards him. 'I think you just pushed your luck a little too far,' he said softly.

'What do you think, Vanessa?'

She couldn't have answered to save her life. Her head was spinning with the suddenness of it all. She was caught like an animal in a trap, capable of nothing except resignation to its fate. She watched with a kind of fascination as Max's head bent towards hers, his purpose all too clear. Then hard lips were on hers, forcing, demanding a response. Logic told her to suffer his embrace passively in the hope that he would let her go when he got no reaction from her, but logic was nothing to do with flesh and blood. It was impossible to deny her pleasure at his touch, and she did not try, her mouth opening beneath the assertion of his, her body moulding itself closer against him.

She made no protest as his hands released her blouse from the confining band of her skirt and stroked the bare flesh beneath it. He reached upwards to caress her breasts and they swelled with desire at his touch. Her whole body seemed to come alive, engulfed in a wave of passionate need that cried out for fulfilment. No man had ever brought her to such a state, half floating, half drowning in a tide of feeling that threatened to overwhelm her.

Then as suddenly as he had seized her, he let her go again. Vanessa staggered back from him, weak with reaction. Not that he was unmoved. He was breathing hard and there was a tautness about the firm line of his mouth that suggested that he too was having difficulty in keeping his feelings in check.

'You asked for that,' he said thickly. 'You all but sat up and begged for it. So don't expect an apology, because you won't get one.'

She took a deep breath, trying to steady herself and shake the reaction from her trembling limbs. 'I don't want——' she began.

'What you want is immaterial as far as I'm concerned. But don't try and tell me that you didn't want me just now.'

'I hate you!'

'Was that what it was?' he scoffed. 'Come off it, Vanessa. You were desperate for me. You didn't want me to stop. But you won't admit that, will you? You haven't got that much honesty about you.'

She was silent. He was right, of course. He could have done anything with her and she would not have protested. On the contrary, she would have been a more than willing partner. Her cheeks burned with shame at the thought of how freely she had offered herself, invitation in every line of her body.

'Women like you sicken me at times,' Max added coldly.

'Really? A fine way you've got of showing it!'

'I wasn't in danger of losing control,' he said.

She wasn't altogether sure of that. 'Then why?' she asked.

'I wanted to teach you a lesson. One that you wouldn't forget in a hurry.'

'And what was that?'

His smile was faintly cruel. 'That sometimes, Vanessa, you can't have just what you want. It would have been all too easy to ignore the come-on signals, the advancing and backing-off that's been going on. I'm not blind, you know. You've been out to get some kind of reaction from me ever since we met, haven't you?'

'No,' she said fiercely, although a voice inside her acknowledged that it was true. She knew that she had been playing with fire from the beginning, but something had driven her on to ignore the danger, even to take pleasure in it.

He shrugged. 'All right, deny it, if it makes you feel

any better. We both know I'm right, though.' He looked down at his stained clothes and frowned. 'And you know what to expect if you ever try any tricks like that again.'

'I won't,' she vowed, as much to herself as to him.

He walked to the door, obviously intending to go and change. 'Remember that in future and we may reach some kind of understanding.'

Vanessa doubted that very much. Left alone, she slumped back against the sofa feeling totally drained. Then, with determination, she forced herself to get up and go back to the desk. It seemed that she still had a job. Whatever her employer thought about her, it appeared that his opinion of her typing skills was unaltered. She sat down and automatically tidied some papers, a good three-quarters of her brain alert for the sound of Max's return to the living room. Had she got the nerve to ignore him and what had taken place between them? Forget it, she couldn't, of that she was sure.

But her shakily assumed poise was not tested after all. The bedroom door opened and closed and she tensed nervously. But then the front door slammed behind him. A few minutes later she heard the snarl of the Maserati as he drove away, accelerating down the road with a fine disregard for such things as speed limits. Clearly Max had taken as much as he could stand from her this morning.

Vanessa looked at the page in front of her and realised that she had been typing total gibberish for the last five minutes. She noticed that her hand shook as she reached to pull the paper from the machine and start again. Shock, she thought. It took one that way sometimes. She got up, went to her employer's well-stocked drinks cabinet and poured herself a generous slug of brandy. It was the first alcohol that she had touched since the night of the party. After that episode she had almost sworn off drink altogether. But this was strictly medicinal. She took a cautious sip, then another, and felt better as a comforting warmth resulted.

Rebellion stirred within her. Darn Max Anderson! Just who did he think he was to treat her the way he had done and expect to get away with it? He had claimed that he wanted to teach her a lesson. What right had he to direct her education? She wasn't a child any more. If he had still been there instead of running away from her like that, she could have told him as much. She took another sip of Dutch courage and then put the glass down with a sigh. 'Face the truth,' she told herself firmly. 'You wouldn't have had the nerve to do anything of the kind. And your best course now is to say nothing more about it and hope that he doesn't either. What kind of fool are you, Vanessa Herbert, to think you can take him on and win?'

She went back to work, but found it hard to keep her mind on what she was doing. Max's face kept coming between her and the page and she ruined sheet after sheet of paper. Lucky that he wasn't there to see her, she thought wryly, as she emptied the wastepaper basket for the umpteenth time. The telepone rang twice and each time she tensed as she stretched out a hand to answer it, wondering if it was Max. She was half disappointed to find it wasn't although she couldn't think why she should be. But her feelings where Max was concerned were too difficult to analyse, the way she was this morning.

She did another hour's work and then broke for lunch. She was in the kitchen, surveying the contents of the fridge in a lacklustre fashion and trying to work up some enthusiasm for a meal, when she heard the front door open. So Max was back. Then she realised her mistake. That quick, light step was not Max's purposeful tread. Vanessa spun round as the intruder paused at the living room door and then came on to the kitchen.

'Max? Where are you hiding yourself?'

If the visitor was surprised to find himself confronted by a strange female wielding a wicked-looking bread-knife in one hand he concealed it admirably. He was as tall as Max and, like him, in his mid to late thirties. But there the resemblance ended. This man was rake-thin and slightly built and had a mop of untidy blond hair that fell in front of his eyes. Certainly not a potential burglar Vanessa relaxed

He put up a hand and smoothed his hair out of his eyes, revealing a friendly blue gaze that was frankly appreciative as he said, 'Was the knife intended for Max, or did you think I was the neighbourhood strong-arm guy?'

She laughed a little self consciously and lowered the weapon. 'You rather took me by surprise. I grabbed the first thing that came to hand.'

'I'm Daniel Jensen. For his sins Max is a friend of mine.' He held out a hand and she shook it, wincing slightly at the bone-crushing strength of his grasp.

She detected a faint transatlantic drawl. 'American?' she guessed.

'Canadian—careful, we're touchy about that.' He didn't look too put out at the mistake. Vanessa warmed to him. 'But I'm almost an Englishman by adoption, I'm over here so often. Max lends me this place when he's not using it. I get sick of hotel rooms.'

'So you've got a key to the flat.' She was relieved to solve that mystery.

'Sure.' He grinned at her. 'Did you think my education included a course in breaking and entering?'

She remembered her manners rather belatedly. 'I'm Vanessa Herbert.'

'And you're Max's——'

'Secretary,' she supplied hastily, anxious that there should be no misunderstandings on that score.

'I see.' And he'd noted her tone too. 'And right now you're calling him all the names under the sun for not telling you to expect me, right?'

'Something like that,' she admitted ruefully. 'He might have mentioned it.'

'Blame me, not him. He didn't know. It's only a quick trip this time. I'm en route to Europe and had a few hours to kill between planes. Waiting round airports isn't my kind of fun, so I thought I'd stop by and see Max. I tried calling from the airport and couldn't get through, so I reckoned I'd come over anyway and hope to find him here. I'm sorry if I startled you.'

'It's all right.' Vanessa smiled at him.

'Where is Max?' he asked. 'Is he around?'

'He left a while ago. I've no idea where he was going.' That didn't sound like a conscientious secretary, but she couldn't help it. 'You could try the television centre. Or he might have gone to Fleet Street to his office there.' She frowned with the effort of working out how to track him down. 'I could phone round, if you like? How much time have you got?'

'Forget it. There's no problem. I'll see him next time I'm over. And I've just thought of a much better idea.' Daniel Jensen dismissed her suggestions with a wave of one large, bony hand.

'Well?'

He rubbed his stubbly chin and grimaced. 'I'm just off an overnight flight from the States and in no fit state to escort a lady anywhere at the moment, but I look quite presentable when I'm cleaned up, believe me. I've got my overnight bag with me. How about me grabbing a quick shave and shower and taking you out to lunch instead of Max? You're a whole lot easier on the eye to a jaded traveller like me than he would be, I'm telling you.'

'I don't know what to say.'

'Say yes and make me happy,' he said persuasively.

Vanessa was tempted by the offer. From the little she had seen of him so far, she liked Daniel Jensen. He was friendly and uncomplicated and an hour or so in his company would do far more to revive her flagging feelings than brooding alone in the flat. But what if Max came back and found her gone? What would his reaction be? She shuddered to think.

Daniel was looking amused. 'Is it such a heavy decision to make? You look as if the cares of the world had suddenly descended on you. I don't bite, you know.'

'I'm sure you don't.'

'Then what's the problem? A girl doesn't usually take so long to make her mind up when I ask her out to lunch.'

She laughed. 'It's no reflection on you, I assure you.'

He gave an exaggerated sigh of relief. 'That's great. I was beginning to wonder.'

'Let's compromise, shall we?' she said. 'You go and have your shower and I'll make us some lunch here. Then, if Max gets back before you have to leave, you'll be able to see him.' And he won't be able to pitch into me for disappearing without his august permission, she added silently. What a coward she was where that man was concerned!

Daniel shrugged. 'That's fine by me, if it's not creating too much trouble for you.'

'You haven't sampled my cooking yet,' she teased him. 'I might be offering you beans on toast.'

'And, if you are, I'm sure I'll enjoy every mouthful in such delightful company.'

'You're not by any chance flirting with me, are you,

Mr Jensen?' she asked him.

'Trying to,' he admitted with a grin. 'And the name's Daniel, so use it, will you?' He turned for the door. 'Give me ten minutes. O.K.?'

'Fine,' she agreed, and set to work.

By the time he reappeared, looking considerably fresher for a wash and a change of clothes, Vanessa had two steaks sizzling on the stove. Max had probably intended them for an intimate supper with his woman of the moment, but that couldn t be helped She made a quick salad with an oil and lemon dressing. There was fruit for pudding and cheese and biscuits if he wanted them. Not a very ambitious meal, but it was quick to prepare and it smelled appetising.

'Mm. Something looks good.' Daniel slipped a casual arm round her waist.

She slapped his hand and twisted free. 'Don't distract the cook at work. Your steak will be a charred ruin if you don't watch out.' She wasn't worried. She'd met men like Daniel before and knew exactly how to handle them. 'Would you like wine with your meal? You'd better look at Max's store and see if there's anything there you fancy.'

'I fancy what's on view at the kitchen stove,' he said with heavy gallantry. 'But I can see that I'm getting nowhere fast.'

'Got it in one,' she answered, and he shrugged good-humouredly. He went to inspect Max's wine collection, stored at the other end of the kitchen.

'I think this will do nicely.' He selected a bottle and held it up for her approval.

'Whatever you like. I'm no expert,' she told him, and searched for a corkscrew for him.

Vanessa made no claims to being a Cordon Bleu cook, but she felt reasonably pleased with her efforts when they sat down to eat, and Daniel praised her fulsomely. They had elected to stay in the kitchen. There didn't seem much point in taking everything into the living room and, in any case, the table in there was pretty well occupied with books and papers that Max had left there. It was more than her life was worth to move them and hope to put them back in the right order.

'So tell me about yourself,' said Daniel, as he filled her wine glass.

'What sort of things do you want to know?'

'Everything.'

'That's a tall order.' She smiled at him, relaxed in his company. 'Well, I'm footloose and fancy free. I'm really an actress, but I'm doing secretarial work while I'm——'

'Between jobs?' he suggested carefully, with a tact that she found surprising.

'Resting, as we say over here,' she responded with a laugh. Somehow she could joke about it to Daniel. 'I was just in a terrible flop in the West End. It was going to make me a star, only it didn't.' She pulled a face. 'Something will come up soon, I hope. In the meantime what I earn here pays the rent.'

'And do you like working for Max?'

'It's a job,' she said carefully.

'That means you don't.' He looked amused. 'Well, wonders will never cease!'

She didn't pretend to misunderstand him. 'Terrible, isn't it? I should think half the women in London would swap places with me, if they had the chance. Do you think there's something wrong with me?'

'Not from where I'm sitting, Vanessa.' He studied her with frank admiration. 'You look like an angel. You cook like a dream. What more could a man want?'

'Quite a bit more, if his name's Max Anderson,' she

said. 'But we won't go into that.'

'Discreet, too,' he noted. 'Are there no end to your virtues?'

'Stop teasing me, Daniel, and tell me something about yourself. I think it's your turn. What do you do for a living?'

It seemed to her that he paused slightly before answering. 'Oh, I'm just a businessman,' he said.

'High-powered?'

'A real whizz-kid,' he assured her solemnly, and she burst out laughing. In a casual checked shirt and slacks he certainly didn't look like a captain of industry, and she told him as much.

'Appearances are deceptive,' he told her loftily. 'We can't all afford Savile Row suits, you know.' He reached for the wine bottle. 'Hey, you're not drinking. Come on now, keep me company.'

Vanessa complied reluctantly, draining her glass and letting him refill it. 'Red wine in the middle of the day always makes me sleepy,' she explained. 'Goodness knows how I'll manage to work after all this.'

'I'll give you the rest of the day off.'

'Thanks for nothing! You're not my employer.'

'I wish I was. Secretaries don't come looking like you at home. Trust Max to grab you. Are there any more where you came from?'

'They broke the mould after they made me,' she told him.

'I suspected as much.'

Daniel was fun. Vanessa was enjoying herself, responding happily to the outrageous things he said to her and teasing him in her turn. They finished the meal and he insisted on helping her with the washing up.

'When do you have to be back at Heathrow?' Vanessa asked as she dried the final plate vigorously and put down the drying cloth.

'Are you so desperate to get rid of me?' he said in mock offence.

'Far from it. In fact,' she told him impulsively, 'I haven't enjoyed myself so much for ages.'

'I think the same goes for me as well.' He turned and planted a light kiss on her upturned cheek. 'How about letting me give you dinner some time and thanking you properly?'

She paused within the circle of his arm, looking up at him as she wondered what to say. Instinct told her to accept, but what would Max make of it, if he found out? Were her employer's friends out of bounds where she was concerned?

She discovered what Max thought sooner than she expected as a cool voice came from behind them. 'This is all very cosy. I'm glad to see you're keeping busy, Vanessa.'

CHAPTER SIX

MAX was standing in the doorway, looking distinctly unamused by the little scene that was being played out before him. Vanessa sprang away from the man beside her as if his touch had suddenly become red hot.

'Hi, Max.' Daniel was the only one of the three who seemed totally relaxed in the situation. She suspected that it was probably one that he had taken part in many times before. 'How's everything going with you?'

For a moment Vanessa held her breath as it seemed that Max was not going to respond to the cheerful greeting. Then, with the faintest of shrugs, he answered, 'I'm fine. And you're enjoying life as usual, I see. Dan, with all the women in London to choose from, do you have to distract my secretary from her work?'

'I never could resist a pretty face.'

'I realised that a long time ago.'

'And she wasn't complaining, were you, Vanessa?'

A glacial gaze turned in her direction. 'I can imagine,' Max said.

Daniel sensed the atmosphere and did his best to put matters right. 'Come on now, Max, there's no need to behave like a bear with a sore head. I turned up out of the blue, gave Vanessa a hell of a fright by walking in on her unannounced and then demanded lunch. What could the poor girl do but play along?'

'Play seems the operative word,' Max agreed dryly. 'I wonder whose idea the after lunch entertainment was?' A cold look in her direction made it clear that he had supplied his own answer to that question. He appeared

94

to dismiss the matter from his mind. 'Well, come on through with me. I want to hear all the news.' He waved Daniel towards the living room and, as the other man went past him and into the passage, turned to follow him, saying casually over his shoulder as he did so, 'We'll have some coffee as soon as you can make it. I could use some.'

Vanessa presumed the remark was addressed to her. 'Have you eaten? Shall I make you some sandwiches?'

'Oh, spare me the fuss. I'm not Daniel,' he said rudely. 'And Vanessa——'

'Yes?'

'Don't think the matter's closed, will you?' He went into the other room and shut the door firmly behind him.

She hadn't time to think. He would want to know where the coffee was if it didn't appear pronto. She rushed round and, when it was ready, put the cups on a tray with milk and sugar and carried it to the door. It seemed silly to knock, but perhaps what they were discussing was private? She compromised by rattling the handle loudly before she opened the door, glad she had done so when she realised that she had clearly interrupted a serious discussion of some kind.

Daniel broke off in the middle of some point that he was making and gave her a slightly conspiratorial smile that raised her spirits. She wondered whether to serve the coffee, but Max waved her away impatiently as soon as she had put the tray down. As she left, shutting the door carefully behind her, she heard the discussion resume.

She went back to the kitchen and busied herself putting dishes and utensils away. When the room was restored to its usual spotless state she sat down disconsolately on a chair and speculated on what would happen when Daniel left. The arctic look Max had given her boded ill for their future relations. Clearly he had decided not to embarrass his friend by making an issue of it while he was still there. But the reckoning was only postponed. Vanessa shivered slightly, wondering what form retribution would take.

She had over an hour in which to drum her heels and grow heartily bored of inactivity. She wished she had a book to read or even some work to do, but everything was out of reach in the living room. She went to the window and watched pigeons mating on the roof of the houses opposite. Lucky creatures. They didn't have an irascible employer monitoring their activities.

She was still standing there, her mind only half on the scene before her, when she heard the living room door open again and the sound of Daniel's voice making leaving noises. She wondered if he would be allowed to say goodbye to her. It had been fun to meet him, almost worth the hot water she had got in with Max.

'I'll be off now.' Daniel appeared at the kitchen door with a smile for her. 'Thanks again. That was a fine lunch you gave me.'

'I'm glad you enjoyed it,' she said with sincerity. 'Shall I get you a taxi for the airport?'

'No need, Max is driving me in. See you again, Vanessa.' With a cheerful wave Daniel was gone and Max with him, the latter not deigning to say anything to her. The front door slammed behind them.

Vanessa collected the coffee cups and washed them, then drifted back into the living room. Perhaps if she had some beautiful typing to show Max on his return things might not be so bad. But it was useless. Her fingers were all thumbs. She might as well not have made the effort, she thought dismally.

When five o'clock came Max had still not returned. She tidied up the desk and fetched her coat, wondering whether she should stay or go. If this had been a

What made Marge burn the toast and miss her favorite soap opera?

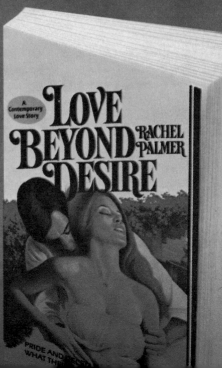

A Contemporary Love Story

LOVE BEYOND DESIRE

RACHEL PALMER

...At his touch, her body felt a familiar wild stirring, but she struggled to resist it. This is not love, she thought bitterly.

PRIDE AND
WHAT THE

A SUPERROMANCE™
the great new romantic novel she never wanted to end.
And it can be yours
FREE!

She never wanted it to end. And neither will you. From the moment you begin... *Love Beyond Desire,* your **FREE** introduction to the newest series of bestseller romance novels, **SUPERROMANCES**.

You'll be enthralled by this powerful love story... from the moment Robin meets the dark, handsome Carlos and finds herself involved in the jealousies, bitterness and secret passions of the Lopez family. Where her own forbidden love threatens to shatter her life.

Your FREE *Love Beyond Desire* is only the beginning. A subscription to **SUPERROMANCES** lets you look forward to a long love affair. Month after month, you'll receive four love stories of heroic dimension. Novels that will involve you in spellbinding intrigue, forbidden love and fiery passions.

You'll begin this series of sensuous, exciting contemporary novels... written by some of the top romance novelists of the day... with four each month.

And this big value... each novel, almost 400 pages of compelling reading... is yours for only $2.50 a book. Hours of entertainment for so little. Far less than a first-run movie or Pay-TV. Newly published novels, with beautifully illustrated covers, filled with page after page of delicious escape into a world of romantic love... delivered right to your home.

A compelling love story of mystery and intrigue... conflicts and jealousies... and a forbidden love that threatens to shatter the lives of all involved with the aristocratic Lopez family.

↳ **Mail this card today for your FREE gifts.**

TAKE THIS BOOK
AND TOTE BAG FREE!

Mail to: **SUPERROMANCE**
2504 W. Southern Avenue, Tempe, Arizona 85282

YES, please send me FREE and without any obligation, my **SUPERROMANCE** novel, *Love Beyond Desire*. If you do not hear from me after I have examined my FREE book, please send me the 4 new **SUPERROMANCE** books every month as soon as they come off the press. I understand that I will be billed only $2.50 per book (total $10.00). There are no shipping and handling or any other hidden charges. There is no minimum number of books that I have to purchase. In fact, I may cancel this arrangement at any time. *Love Beyond Desire* and the tote bag are mine to keep as FREE gifts even if I do not buy any additional books.

134-CIS-KAF6

Name	(Please Print)
Address	Apt. No.
City	
State	Zip

Signature   (If under 18, parent or guardian must sign.)

PRINTED IN U.S.A.

SUPERROMANCE ™

**EXTRA BONUS
MAIL YOUR ORDER
TODAY AND GET A
FREE TOTE BAG
FROM SUPERROMANCE.**

← Mail this card today for your FREE gifts.

normal day, she would have left promptly. But it wasn't. Hesitating, she hung on for another half hour and then made up her mind to leave and hang the consequences. If Max Anderson thought she was going to wait for him like a schoolgirl expecting her punishment, then he had another think coming! And there was always the faint hope that by tomorrow he might have forgotten that she had annoyed him by entertaining Daniel so wholeheartedly.

She caught herself holding her breath in suspense as she left the flat and pressed the button for the lift. What if she met him on her way out and had to be dragged ignominiously back? She didn't doubt that he would do precisely that if it suited him. But, for once in this awful day, luck was on her side and she made it safely home.

'Did you have a good day?' Jill had got in before her and was busy in the kitchen when Vanessa got in.

'I think it could best be called patchy.'

When they sat down to their evening meal she expanded on that remark and told her sister what had happened. 'I don't see I could have done anything else but feed the man,' she claimed resentfully. 'I don't know why Max was so cross.'

'Does kissing come under the heading of feeding him?'

'He was kissing me. There's a difference. And anyway, it wasn't anything. Any fool could have seen that.'

'I wouldn't have thought Max Anderson could be described as a fool exactly,' commented Jill.

'He just seems to have a blind spot where I'm concerned. I can't do a thing right,' Vanessa grumbled. 'I'm only surprised he didn't sack me on the spot; he would have enjoyed that. But I suppose he was too much of a hypocrite to make a scene with Daniel Jensen there.'

'Who did you say?'

'Daniel Jensen. Why?'

'Tall, blond, Canadian?'

'Yes. So what?'

Jill was looking at her with round eyes. 'So what? You entertained Daniel Jensen to lunch at the kitchen table?'

'Yes. I just told you so, didn't I? What's the big deal?'

'That must have been a novelty for him. I don't suppose he does that very often.'

'Stop talking in riddles, Jill. Who is the man? Do you know him?'

'The likes of me don't often come into contact with the Daniel Jensens of this world. Vanessa, you must have heard of him.'

'Now you mention it, the name is vaguely familiar.' Vanessa concentrated, but drew a blank. 'Could I have seen a photograph somewhere? Is he famous or something?'

'Infamous, more like. Do you never look at newspapers?'

'Only the theatre pages.'

'He's a financial wizard. Inherited more millions than the average person would know how to spend when he was only a child. When he was old enough to take control he sacked his business advisers and set about things himself. He doubled everything in three years. Or was it trebled?' Jill frowned. 'I can't remember. The empire stretches world-wide and he commutes between Europe and North America the way you or I would catch a number seven bus.'

'Anything else?'

'Oh, it's not all work. I gather he's a bit of a playboy too.'

'That much I'd gathered without reading the papers,' Vanessa said. 'He asked me out to dinner.'

'Are you going?'

'We were rudely interrupted before I had the chance to say yea or nay to the offer,' she replied absently. 'So that's why he said he didn't usually have to wait for an answer to his invitations!'

'I don't think he's used to waiting for anything. People usually jump when he tells them to.'

'I can't see Max jumping for anyone,' Vanessa mused. 'I wonder what the connection is between them. They seemed to be old friends.'

'The theatre's one of his interests, I think,' said Jill. 'He puts up the money for Broadway shows on occasion. And hits the jackpot every time.'

'Worth cultivating, you think?' Vanessa laughed.

'Definitely.'

'If he ever forgives me for not knowing him from Adam,' she said ruefully. 'When will I stop putting my big foot in it? I'll have enough material for a book about it soon.'

'Bear up, love. Things can't get any worse,' Jill consoled her.

'Want to bet?' she said darkly. 'There's tomorrow to get through yet.'

'You sound as if Max will roast you alive!'

'Don't be too sure he won't,' Vanessa muttered, and spent the rest of the evening sunk in despair, alternately dreading her next encounter with Max and wishing it would arrive and be over with.

The storm signals were clearly visible the next morning when she reached the flat. He was waiting for her, a black look on his face.

'It's three minutes past nine,' he said, ostentatiously consulting the heavy gold watch on his wrist. 'Can't you even manage to get here on time?'

'The bus——' she began, and abandoned the excuse

hastily. He wasn't in the mood for listening. 'It won't happen again,' she said.

'You're damned right, it won't. And what about yesterday's little escapade?'

'What about it?' she fenced, playing for time.

'Will that be repeated? Do I have to stay and supervise you to make sure you don't get up to your tricks with anyone else who may drop by unexpectedly?'

'Tell me,' she said sweetly, keeping her temper in check with an almighty effort, 'is it my morals that you're objecting to or the fact that I was entertaining a man in office hours?'

'I pay for your time and I'll decide how you use it. In future you'll keep your hands off my friends.'

'Don't you think Daniel's a bit old to be protected from the likes of me? He's a big boy now. Don't you let him choose his own playmates?'

'He's old enough to know better, certainly,' he conceded. 'I'm surprised he didn't get your measure straight away. Offering to cook lunch for him, indeed! Quite a little *hausfrau*, aren't you?'

'I suppose you'd rather I'd told him you weren't around and sent him packing?'

'It might have been the most sensible course.'

'Sensible for whom?' she asked.

'For you, perhaps. We wouldn't be arguing about it now, if you had.'

'But I didn't.'

'No, of course not. I wouldn't have expected you to do any such thing. A gold-digger like you wouldn't miss a chance like that.' He gave a derisive laugh. 'And you had the gall to call me an opportunist!' He hooked his hands in the belt of his jeans and studied her contemptuously. 'It's a pity I arrived so inopportunely. You hadn't much time to work in. What would have happened if I'd come in half an hour later? I suppose I'd have caught you in my bed with him, would I?'

'You've got a mind like a sewer,' she told him heatedly. 'What makes you think you've the right to talk to me like that?'

'I generally adapt my conversation to the company I keep. You can make what you like of that.'

Her hand went up to slap his face, but he anticipated the action and fended off the blow with ease, grasping her arm cruelly as he did so. 'I've warned you before about that sort of behaviour, but you don't listen, do you?' He twisted her arm behind her back as he jerked her towards him. 'If you persist in behaving like an alley-cat you'll take the consequences.'

'You're so lily-white yourself, of course,' she taunted him.

'Not particularly. But I wouldn't touch what you've got to offer with a bargepole.'

'Who says I'm offering you anything?' she flared.

'No, I haven't got as much to give you as Daniel has.' She tried to reason with him. 'I didn't know who he was.'

'Don't try to pull that one. It won't work.'

'But it's true!'

He ignored her protest, pulling her nearer to him, seemingly without effort. 'Look at me, Vanessa.'

She jerked her head away, rebellious to the last. The hard pressure of his fingers round her arm was painful, but at the same time it sent tremors of awareness down her spine. The clean, male smell of him awakened her senses to his physical attraction for her. It was no use telling herself that he was dangerous and that he despised her. What she felt for him was a purely instinctive reaction that conscious thought could not banish.

'Look at me, Vanessa,' he insisted, and his hand tightened its grip. She obeyed him, meeting the tawny gaze full on with a defiant look of her own.

'You're hurting me,' she said coldly.

'I'm sorry.' He didn't sound it. 'Promise me one thing and I'll let you go.'

'Well?'

'What you get up to in your own time is your own affair, I suppose. But while I'm picking up the tab you'll do what you're paid for. Is that clearly understood?'

'Yes. Perfectly clear.' He let her go and she stood rubbing her arm. 'I could report you to the agency for this,' she told him. 'Assault and battery don't come into the contract as far as I'm aware.'

'Neither does making love in your employer's time,' he retorted. 'Of which we've wasted more than enough already this morning. So you'd better get on with something.'

She glared at him, but deemed it wiser to do as he said.

Max watched her start work and then left. Obviously he didn't intend to carry out his threat of keeping her company to make sure that her behaviour came up to his exacting standards.

For the next few days they treated each other with polite caution, circling around each other carefully if they had occasion to meet. The incident with Daniel lay between them, never mentioned, but somehow always there in the background. Vanessa got on with her work, hoping that the assignment would be over soon. The pages of play script mounted all too slowly for her satisfaction, as Max piled her desk high with other pieces of work that he wanted done. Sometimes she wondered if she would ever get away from him.

It was about ten days later when the phone rang just as she was leaving for home. She was tempted to ignore it, then shrugged and picked it up. If it was Max he'd only accuse her of falling down on the job if he didn't get an answer at a minute to five o'clock.

The voice that met her ears was transatlantic and

vaguely familiar. 'Hi there, Vanessa. I'm glad I caught you.'

'Daniel?'

'The very same. I'm back in London.'

'Max isn't here,' she told him.

'Who said it was Max I wanted? I seem to remember we had a dinner date to fix. Is it still on?'

Vanessa had a feeling that the safe reply to his question would be a polite evasion. Max would no doubt expect that. But he had told her that her private life was her own. And she *liked* Daniel. She threw caution to the winds. 'I'd love to have dinner with you. What day shall we make it?'

'Would it be asking too much of you to say tonight?' he queried. 'Are you free?'

'I did have a pressing appointment at home with the latest Agatha Christie, but I expect I can put it off for you,' she teased.

He laughed. 'That's great. I'll do my best to be equally entertaining, I promise. Give me your address and I'll pick you up. Shall we say round about eight o'clock?'

She gave him the details. 'That'll be fine. I'll look forward to it.'

She gathered her things and rushed for the door. Daniel would be picking her up in exactly three hours. It sounded an age, but if she was going to bath, wash her hair and hunt through her wardrobe to find something suitable to wear, she'd better step on it.

'No egg and chips for me tonight, Jill. Caviar and champagne. My millionaire is taking me out on the town,' she announced to her sister.

'You do have all the luck. Daniel?'

'How many millionaires do you think I know? Of course it's Daniel. Now, be an angel, and help me to choose something to wear. I've got to look presentable and I haven't that much time to work miracles.'

At five to eight Vanessa surveyed herself in the mirror with some satisfaction. She knew she was looking her best. Daniel hadn't said where he was taking her, but she was confident she would pass muster anywhere. The severly cut black evening skirt contrasted well with the white chiffon blouse whose plunging neckline was a mass of layered frills. A band of black velvet round her neck set off the outfit perfectly. Skilful use of make-up emphasised the creamy perfection of her skin and the depths to her dark blue eyes.

'I'll say this for you, Van,' Jill said admiringly as she watched her sister outline her mouth with a deep pink lipstick. 'You don't need expensive clothes and a mass of jewellery to turn yourself into something stunning.'

Vanessa studied herself carefully. 'Partly training, of course. But not bad, not bad at all. And it's just as well I can do without diamonds and the like. I don't suppose they'll ever be within reach of my pay-packet. Not that I'm complaining. Most women who have well-stocked jewellery boxes look a bit like overloaded Christmas trees when they're dressed to kill.'

The door-bell rang. 'He's keen—bang on time. Let me go to the door, Van,' begged Jill. 'I've always wanted to talk to a real live millionaire.'

'Be my guest. I just hope you're not disappointed.'

But it was clear when Jill ushered Daniel into the room that his charm had won her over in the short space of time it took to walk from the door. He was in evening dress, his mop of blond hair brushed tidily back, and she was glad she had made such an effort to look good as his eyes made an appreciative appraisal of her. He accepted a glass of sherry and sat down. Clearly his interest lay with Vanessa, but he was polite enough to chat with evident enjoyment to Jill about her work and life in London. Half an hour passed very pleasantly and then he looked at his watch and suggested that it was time to go.

'The table's booked for nine o'clock and I expect you're ready to eat after a hard day's work for my friend Max.'

'How right you are!' Vanessa got her wrap and they left in the taxi that was still parked patiently outside, its meter clocking up what seemed a phenomenal amount.

'You should have told me you had a cab waiting,' she apologised. 'I wouldn't have taken so long.'

Daniel shrugged. 'It's no great hassle. Usually I hire a car, but it wasn't worth it this time. I got in from Rome this morning and I'm off for the States again tomorrow.'

'That's quite a schedule. And yet you found time to offer me dinner?'

'Any objections? I promise I won't disgrace myself by falling asleep over the table.'

'No. But there must have been a thousand other things you had to do,' she protested.

'Probably,' he agreed. 'But when I look at you right now I can't think of one of them.'

'Oh, you're impossible!' Vanessa laughed, and settled down to enjoy the evening ahead.

He took her to a little French restaurant in Soho where he was obviously well known. 'I wasn't sure of your tastes, so I played safe,' he explained as he seated her in her chair before taking his. He smiled at her. 'Hungry?'

'Starving!'

He handed her the menu and they made their choices known to the waiter who was hovering deferentially. Both elected to start with pâté, following with fish, Vanessa's in a creamy sauce while Daniel preferred his simply grilled with butter.

'I travel so much that I've learnt to stick to plain foods and avoid trouble,' he told her.

'It's a good principle.'

'And well worth relating to other areas. I prefer my women straightforward too.'

Like his friend Max. The thought came unbidden to her mind. 'I'm sorry I didn't recognise you when we first met. You must have thought me an awful fool.'

'There's no need to apologise,' he said easily. 'I was charmed. It's not every day I'm mistaken for a house-breaker.'

'If I'd known who you were I'd have made more effort to——'

'To what? Kowtow to me? It's not what I enjoy, you know. You can't realise how refreshing I found your approach. Being loved for one's bank balance palls after a while.'

'Poor little rich boy,' Vanessa teased him.

'I can see I'll have my work cut out to get any sympathy out of you.' But he was laughing as he said it.

The sweets trolley appeared by their side as if by magic and Vanessa debated at length, unable to make up her mind which delectable gateau to choose.

'The lady will have some of each.' Daniel made the decision for her, taking cheese and biscuits for himself. 'You're a baby, Vanessa, did anyone ever tell you that? You looked like a kid in a candy store just now.'

'I amuse you, do I?' She affected offended dignity. 'You may be used to all this, Daniel Jensen, but I'm not. Struggling actresses don't live your kind of life.'

'Tell me how the other half live,' he invited.

'You wouldn't be interested.'

'Try me and see.'

She gave him a brief sketch of her career to date, recalling humorous incidents that had happened to her and to other people and making light of the hard times that had come in between. He was shrewd enough to fill in the gaps, she sensed that.

'You've enjoyed it so far? You're glad you chose it?' he asked.

'Yes. I wouldn't want to do anything else.'

'Marriage? A family?'

'Oh, in the dim and distant future. But I've no plans for that as yet.'

'Then there's some hope for me?'

'If you play your cards right, we'll see,' she teased him, not taking him too seriously.

'And there's no sign of a job on the horizon at the moment?'

'Not even a glimmer of one. I rang my agent this morning. He says it's a slack time of year, but that's a standard excuse.'

'I could help you, you know, if you'd let me,' offered Daniel.

'No,' she said abruptly, the smile vanishing from her face. She remembered her manners and added hastily, 'That is, thanks, but no, thanks. I'll manage on my own, if you don't mind.'

He looked taken aback. 'What's the matter?' Then his face cleared. 'You think I'm part of the deal, is that it? It's all right, Vanessa. I wasn't expecting any favours in return.'

She frowned. 'No, I don't think you were.'

'Then what's the problem? I'd like to help, believe me.' He reached across the table and took her hand reassuringly. 'Can't you trust me?'

'Yes, but it's not as simple as that,' she began. 'You see——'

'Max has offered to do something, has he? I reckon he's got a lot of clout in the theatre world, if he chooses to use it.'

'He doesn't,' she said baldly. 'At least, not for me.'

'Did you ask him to?' Daniel sounded intrigued.

'I wouldn't ask Max Anderson the time of day,' she told him indignantly. 'I'm sorry to have to say that about someone who's a friend of yours, but that's the way I feel and there's no point trying to hide it.'

'You're not going to stop there, I hope?' Daniel signalled to the waiter to bring them coffee and, when they had been served, returned to the subject. 'Well, what's Max done to get across you?'

'It's a long, rather boring story and I won't weary you with the details. But, as a result, he thinks I'm a scheming little bitch who considers no sacrifice too great in order to get a part, including offering my sexual favours to men who revolt me,' she said bitterly.

'I can't imagine how he got that impression.'

'Then you don't agree with him?' Vanessa asked. It was a relief to find that Daniel was capable of making up his own mind about her and had come to a different conclusion.

'I'd hardly be sitting here with you if I did. Don't worry about that. I know the type. I should do, I've met enough of them over the years. And you're not like that, I can tell. And if he's got any sense at all in that head of his, Max ought to be able of spotting the difference too. But if he can't, that's his hard luck.'

'Thank you,' she said simply. 'It's nice to have a vote of confidence.'

He squeezed her hand. 'I could go on to tell you any number of nice things that I've noticed about you, but I've a strong suspicion you wouldn't believe me.'

'You'd be right too,' Vanessa told him.

'You're a hard girl to please. I can see I'll have to try a different approach with you, if I'm to get anywhere.'

She laughed, relaxing again. 'You're nice, Daniel. Has anyone ever told you that?'

'Frequently,' he grinned. 'But I never get tired of hearing it.'

She aimed a mock blow at him across the table. 'You're also a smooth-talking con man where women are concerned.'

'Reform me,' he suggested wickedly.

'I haven't got time. It would be a life's work.'

'That's what everyone says,' he lamented.

They sat for another hour, laughing and joking, before Vanessa, mindful of work the next day, suggested that it was time to go. 'It's been tremendous fun, but I have to be slaving over a typewriter tomorrow and you've got a long flight ahead of you.'

'Such concern for my welfare,' he mocked her. 'Or are you just worried about the beating Max will give you if you fall asleep at your desk in the morning?'

'You've guessed it.'

He laughed and called for the bill. 'Right. Shall we go?' He helped her on with her wrap and guided her towards the door, his arm protectively round her. 'Next time we'll go somewhere quieter,' he said as they threaded their way through the noisy crowds of after-theatre diners who had just filled the restaurant. 'There's a place I know out at Windsor that I'm sure you'd like.'

'So there's to be a next time, is there?'

'If you'd like that, Vanessa.'

'Very much,' she told him. 'I've enjoyed myself tonight.'

'That's good news.' His arm tightened a fraction round her.

She was concentrating on Daniel rather than where she was going when she stumbled into the back of a chair that was slightly out from its table. 'I'm sorry,' she apologised hastily to its occupant for jarring him.

He turned. 'That's quite all right, Vanessa,' he said coldly.

It was like a shower of icy water in her face. Fortunately Daniel took the initiative. 'Max! I didn't see you come in. Why didn't you come over?'

'You seemed to be fairly engrossed, and I didn't want to intrude.' The words were polite, but there was an edge to them that both she and Daniel registered.

'Darling? Aren't you going to introduce me to your friends?' Max's companion put her oar in, apparently unaware that anything could be wrong. She was an attractive enough girl with shoulder-length copper hair, wearing a tightly fitting dress that looked as if it was held up by will power and nothing else. One slender, red-taloned hand clutched Max's arm in an effort to attract his attention.

He made brief introductions and they exchanged smiles. As if he sensed the tension in Vanessa Daniel made a move away. 'We were just leaving,' he said, stating the obvious.

'I won't keep you, then. I'm sure you'd rather be on your own.' Max made the remark faintly offensive.

'Do you blame me?' Daniel turned it into a joke. 'It's not every day that I meet someone like Vanessa.'

'That's true enough,' Max agreed, the derision in his voice all too evident.

They said goodbye and left. Out on the pavement Vanessa gulped in the cool night air with relief while Daniel left her to find a taxi. He was back in a moment.

'There's the test of a good escort—finding a cab in thirty seconds flat!'

She managed a weak smile. 'Yes. Look, Daniel, there's no need for you to escort me all the way home. I'll be fine, really I will.'

He gave her a keen look. 'You'd rather be on your own.' It was a statement, not a question.

'Yes.'

'O.K., if that's what you want. But, Vanessa——'

'Yes?' She paused with her hand on the door of the cab, her face turned enquiringly towards him.

'Don't let the last five minutes spoil the rest of the evening for you.'

She warmed to him for his understanding. Daniel Jensen was no fool, she realised, when it came to human relationships. She reached up and kissed him, and the touch of his lips against hers was strangely comforting. 'I won't,' she promised. Then she got quickly in the cab and was driven away.

CHAPTER SEVEN

VANESSA had thought that she would spend a sleepless night worrying about Max and his reaction to her outing with his friend. After all, he had as good as warned her off Daniel. In the event, however, she fell asleep as soon as her head touched the pillow, and, if her dreams were filled with her employer's avenging figure, she was not aware of it. She woke early next morning and lay for a moment, luxuriating in the bright sunshine that streamed through the window. Last night had been fun. She wondered if Daniel would really want to repeat the experience. He had seemed to enjoy it, but she was under no illusions about his attitude to women. If someone else came along, she had an idea she would be ditched pretty quickly.

The phone rang shrilly, shattering the early morning silence. As she roused herself to get up and answer it she heard the pad of her sister's feet outside and sank back with relief.

'Vanessa! It's for you. Daniel, I think,' Jill shouted, and thumped on the door. Galvanised into sudden activity, Vanessa grabbed her dressing gown and ran to the living room to take the call.

'Were you sleeping the sleep of the innocent?' he asked her wickedly. 'I was afraid you might be.'

'What else would I be doing at'—Vanessa consulted the clock on the table beside her—'at six-thirty in the morning?'

'I could make a few suggestions, but I won't.'

'Stop teasing me,' she commanded him. 'Where are you? You sound very bright-eyed and bushy-tailed.'

'At the airport. I'll be taking off in half an hour. I rang to thank you for a very pleasant evening, although perhaps you're wishing I hadn't got you out of bed to do so.'

She laughed. 'I'll survive the experience. I enjoyed last night too.'

'I'll be back again next week. Perhaps we can get together again?'

'Perhaps,' she agreed cautiously. It wouldn't do to sound too eager. That only put men off in her limited experience.

They spoke for a little longer and then Daniel rang off. Thoroughly awake now, Vanessa wandered into the kitchen to make a cup of tea and took a cup in to Jill.

'When's the wedding?' her sister asked jokingly. 'You could do worse than supply me with a millionaire for a brother-in-law. Especially if he's as nice as Daniel seemed to be.'

'I'll warn you you'll wait a long time if you're hoping for that to happen. Daniel's just amusing himself. He's not serious. I'd be a fool to think that he was.'

But if Daniel was only playing with her, he certainly knew how to make a girl feel wanted, she decided. A large bouquet arrived for her just as she was leaving Jill's flat and another was reposing in Max's living room when she arrived there.

'Your admirer seems to have something to thank you for.' Max indicated the card that was attached to the flowers.

She ignored the innuendo in his voice, burying her head in the roses and taking a deep breath of their heady perfume. 'My favourite flowers. I wonder how he knew?'

'Red roses for true love,' Max sneered. 'I believe they're what Daniel usually sends his women. While the affair lasts, of course.'

She refused to let herself get upset by his cynical tone. 'I expect he does,' she agreed. 'But it's a nice gesture.'

'Don't take it too seriously, that's all.'

'Don't tell me you're trying to save me some heartache? I wouldn't have thought you were capable of that sort of generous action.'

'I'm not,' he said curtly. 'Anyway, as you haven't a heart to break, it's superfluous advice, isn't it?'

He was looking rather less than his usual immaculate self this morning as if he had gone to bed with the whisky bottle for company and had passed a restless night as a consequence. She wondered if his companion of last night had decided that she had had enough of his bad temper. In the mood that she and Daniel had left him in, Vanessa could hardly blame her.

He was dressed in black cords and a T-shirt, but the dark hair was rumpled as if it hadn't seen a comb yet this morning and he hadn't shaved. The rough, dark stubble on his cheeks gave him a vaguely piratical air, Vanessa thought. Alert and freshly groomed, he spelt attraction to a woman, but now he exuded a brooding sensuality that stirred her senses even as she recognised its danger for her.

'I'll make some coffee for you,' she said briskly, deliberately dispelling the mood, and went to the kitchen, taking the roses with her to put in some water until she could take them home.

He followed her and stood leaning against the door-jamb, watching her as she worked, his eyes narrowed and expressionless. She wondered what he was thinking. It was probably better that she didn't know.

'So Daniel gave you a good time last night?' he asked her with heavy emphasis.

'Yes, thank you.' She wouldn't rise to the bait. Let him imagine whatever he liked; it was no concern of hers.

'You got on with him?' he persisted.

'Yes. Is that so surprising?'

'He's a friend of mine.'

'Fortunately not all your friends share your personality,' she snapped. 'Daniel's not like you.'

'No, not at all. And he's an attractive man by your standards, isn't he? His pockets are very well lined, which compensates for a deal of faults. He knows how to spend it too. But I expect you've already discovered that.'

He was needling her deliberately, she suspected. She shrugged. 'I suppose there's no point denying it.'

'Not much. I know what you're like.'

She laughed in his face. 'You may think you do. I'd say otherwise myself.'

'I know all I need to know, let's put it like that.'

'Scared?' she taunted him. 'Are you afraid I'll get my money-digging claws into you when I've finished with Daniel?'

'You'd find you'd met your match if you did anything of the kind.'

Vanessa didn't doubt it. He would be a formidable opponent. 'As I've told you before, I'm not interested. So you can count your blessings, can't you?' She poured a mug of strong black coffee for him and banged it down on the table 'There's your coffee. You look as if you need it.'

He strolled into the room and took it, the capable brown hands cradling it as if savouring its warmth. 'Are you trying to manage me, Vanessa?' he asked softly.

'I don't think I'd get very far if I did.'

'There's an admission of defeat.'

'If you like.'

'You're very accommodating this morning. What's wrong with you?' He took a gulp of coffee and studied her narrowly over the rim of the mug. 'Have I Daniel to thank for this new biddable quality in you?'

'Perhaps I'm determined not to argue with you. Anyway,' she said dismissively, 'you hardly look up to dealing with me just at the moment. I'll let you gather your strength again.'

'I don't think I need to do that.' Max put the coffee mug down. 'Come here.'

'No.' She backed away.

'Playing games again?'

She registered a sudden flicker of devilment in his eyes. 'Leave me alone,' she said.

'There's one lesson that you haven't learned yet, Vanessa.'

'And what's that?'

'Never to underestimate the strength of your opponent,' he told her as he closed the distance between them in a couple of strides. He cornered her by the window and pinned her mercilessly against its frame.

'Max! People will see us,' she protested.

'Let them,' he said carelessly, and kissed her.

The harshness of his bristled cheeks grazed hers as his lips sought and found her mouth, delighting her with his touch as he explored its moist sweetness. Instinct told her to melt against him, to abandon herself to the kind of mindless rapture that had taken hold of her when he had kissed her before. It would be all too easy to give in.

But that was what he wanted her to do. Some remnants of sanity remained and struggled for control. Max was only proving a point; that was all the embrace meant to him. He wanted her to submit so that he could demonstrate the power that he had over her. Just as he had demonstrated to hundreds of women before her.

The thoughts whirled round in her head while the insistent pressure of his lips argued in another direction entirely.

For once the magic wasn't going to work, she told herself. But it was hard to resist as his mouth left hers and burnt a tantalising trail of kisses to her ear. The feel of him nibbling gently at the lobe was almost more than she could bear, and the urge to respond took hold of her, weakening her resistance and drugging her senses.

'No!' She made a sudden supreme effort and surprised him, wrenching herself free and facing him with flushed cheeks and heaving breasts. 'I don't want you.'

He took a step towards her. 'I'll make you want me.'

'No. Oh, you can subdue me physically, I'll grant you. You're strong enough to rape me here on the kitchen floor if it suits you. Is that what you want?' she asked contemptuously. 'I thought you only liked willing women?'

'You go too far sometimes, Vanessa,' he said, his face dark with anger. 'I've told you that before for all the notice you've taken of it.'

'And so do you,' she retorted. 'A good deal too far. What's the matter, Max? Can't you bear the thought of Daniel succeeding where you've failed?'

His fists clenched with rage and she felt a sudden frisson of fear snake down her spine. Perhaps she *had* gone too far. But she had no intention of apologising, come what might.

He checked his temper with obvious effort. 'Let's leave it at that, shall we? Otherwise I might do something we may both regret.'

He slammed out of the flat ten minutes later. Vanessa didn't know where he was going and she didn't much care. She applied herself to work with superhuman dedication. The sooner the wretched play script was finished the better as far as she was concerned. She took out the worst of her fury on her typewriter keys, achieving a neatness and accuracy that normally escaped her.

The rest of the week passed without incident. Max's manners to her were impeccable, if rather chilly and distant. He was obviously steering clear of trouble. Vanessa acknowledged a faint feeling of disappointment at his attitude. At least their battles brought a little spice to an otherwise fairly uneventful life. She pestered Jonathan for news of work, but he told her that he had nothing for her. In a sudden burst of enthusiasm she had some more photographs taken of herself and sent them, with details of her career to date, to everyone that she thought might have a part to offer her. She might just as well not have bothered. She received only one acknowledgment that promised to 'bear in mind' that she was free for engagements.

If it had not been for Daniel's daily phone calls from the States her spirits might well have taken a dive. After the first call, which was adroitly fielded by an icily polite Max, he took the hint and rang her outside office hours. What it did to his own business schedule she had no idea, but, taking into account the time difference, she imagined that he must have interrupted quite a few late morning appointments and business lunches in order to reach her.

'These calls must be costing you a fortune,' she protested half heartedly to him when he had stayed talking for nearly an hour, chatting and teasing her about everything under the sun.

'I've got a fortune, haven't I? Who's worrying?' Daniel replied. 'You're the first woman to tell me I'm extravagant when I'm spending money on her. Hey, did you get the roses?'

Another enormous bunch of flowers had arrived two days after the first ones. They were running out of vases to put them all in. 'You spoil me, Daniel,' she said.

'Absence makes the heart——'

'Grow fonder of someone else,' she finished the tag for him.

'It's not true. I can't wait to see you again. Save next Friday evening for me, will you?'

She agreed and put the phone down, smiling a little to herself. She wasn't quite sure how she felt about Daniel yet. It was too new, too uncertain. Perhaps she'd find out more when she saw him again.

'Not Daniel?' Jill asked with a knowing look, coming into the room at that point.

'Mm. Persistent, isn't he?'

'Could it come to anything serious?'

'For him?'

'For you.'

'I'm not sure, Jill.'

'Try going out with someone else. You might get Daniel into a better perspective.'

'Yes, I think you're right. Would you like to conjure some men out of thin air for me?' she asked her sister.

'You've never had any trouble in the past,' she replied dryly. 'Do your own hunting, Van.'

'A party would be nice. I'll ask around and see if anyone I know is in town and feeling social.'

But she didn't need to, as it happened. By a happy accident she bumped into a drama school friend she hadn't seen for years while she was out doing the Saturday shopping in Hampstead High Street and got invited to a party that the other girl was holding that evening.

'I'm shopping for food right now,' Lydia told her. She was a bubbly blonde with a zany sense of humour and, as far as Vanessa remembered, a very real acting talent. 'And I'm in funds for once. I've got a small part in the latest Ayckbourn play that'll run for ever and I've had two or three television pieces come up lately. How about you?'

Vanessa mentioned her one brief West End appearance and got ready sympathy. 'Darling, how awful for you! But something will come along soon. It's bound to.'

'So they say, but nothing does.'

'It will. Look, love, I must dash. The flat hasn't been cleaned for a thousand years and it'll take me the rest of the day to get it halfway to decent. I'm dying to catch up on all the news, though. Come early tonight and then we can have a good talk. You can help me with the food too, if you don't mind.'

'Of course not.' Vanessa noted down the address. 'It's only a stone's throw away from where I am. I'm surprised we haven't bumped into each other before now.'

'Are you in digs?'

'My sister's flat.'

'Bring her too, if you like. The more the merrier. 'Bye!' Lydia was gone, swinging the two bags of groceries in her hands to the imminent peril of the passers by, before Vanessa could explain that Jill was away for the weekend.

She found herself humming snatches of a current pop hit as she showered and got ready that evening. Lydia had been famous for her parties in drama school days. However cramped or unsuitable the surroundings had been her bright personality had ensured that everything went with a swing. Lydia's philosophy of life had been vastly different from her own even then, Vanessa reflected.

'The way I see it, you've got to make the most of your chances,' she had told Vanessa many times, and she had always done exactly that, never averse to buttering up people she actively disliked in the faint hope that they might be persuaded to do something to help her.

'But how can you?' the younger Vanessa had protested once after a party when she had seen her friend disappear into the bedroom with another of the guests, an influential casting director.

'Quite easily, darling. I close my eyes and think about my career. I don't have any scruples about what I'm doing—they're for fools. It's a crowded profession and I'm levelling the odds in my favour, that's all. Of course, it makes it easier if they're good-looking!'

'I can imagine.'

But not all of them had been anything approaching good-looking. Lydia wouldn't have worried about Sam Galveston, Vanessa reflected bitterly. She would have come to some kind of amicable agreement with him and probably ended up with a nice little part in his latest series. She shuddered at the thought of the man. If Lydia was prepared to suffer that kind of mauling in order to further her career, she was welcome to it.

She chose a fairly casual outfit, but one that suited her nonetheless, a dusky pink cotton skirt of a swirly Indian design, coupled with a matching blouse that was gathered at the neck with a collection of tiny bells that jangled attractively as she moved about. A silver bangle, borrowed from Jill's jewellery box, hung on her wrist and she wore strappy silver sandals, a replacement pair that she had bought for those she had lost so disastrously. Usually she had her hair up, but tonight some fancy caused her to leave it hanging straight past her shoulders in a heavy blue-black cloud that somehow accentuated the small-boned delicacy of her face. Her make-up differed from her normal standards too. She ringed her eyes with kohl, making them seem twice their actual size, and dusted her cheeks with a silvery powder that gave them an exotic sheen.

She inspected the final picture critically. Definitely a bit of a contrast from the workaday Vanessa, she decided. And that was no bad thing. For once she was sick of her conventional image. After all, she was an actress, wasn't she? A bohemian creature who inhabited a world vastly different from the mass of nine-to-five workers with their grey clothes and grey, ordered lives. Vanessa pulled a face at herself in the mirror. Most of those office workers she was dismissing as sober and boring probably led more interesting lives than she did herself at the moment.

She grabbed a silver evening purse, stuffed a handkerchief and her keys inside it, and, taking her coat, left the flat. The address Lydia had given her was only ten minutes walk away and it was pleasant on a mild night like this one. Somehow Hampstead never seemed like part of London, more a little village in its own right, bordered by the vast green spaces of the Heath. Vanessa could hear the night birds calling and then the sound of some predator, a fox perhaps, in the undergrowth as she walked along by the area that, in the daytime, was always filled with people enjoying themselves. Sometimes they flew kites round here on Sunday mornings, she remembered. She really must come up here for a brisk walk one weekend instead of lounging around the flat watching television.

It was a basement flat down some steps and through some jungly garden and had an old-fashioned bell pull by the door which sounded harshly when Vanessa used it. Lydia appeared with a bright plastic apron round her waist.

'Darling, you've come in the nick of time.' She ushered her across the doorstep and into a large, high-ceilinged living room that bore signs of a hasty clear-up that hadn't altogether succeeded. A pile of books and magazines sat drunkenly by the side of the shabby sofa and a collection of dirty coffee mugs was standing in the middle of the floor, obviously just rooted out from various corners of the room. Dust lay thickly on every available surface.

'In time for what?' Vanessa asked, knowing all too well. So much for a cosy chat about old times. She should have remembered Lydia's capacity for heaping work on to the shoulders of her friends, willing or not.

'The first people are expected in half an hour and look at the place!' Lydia spread her hands out dramatically. She gave an engaging smile. 'I don't suppose you could help a bit, could you? I meant to do it, but I fell asleep this afternoon.'

'We'd better buckle to, hadn't we?' There was no point arguing over it. 'How's the food going?'

'I was just doing that. If you could do a bit of washing up or something . . .' The other girl's voice tailed off as she headed for the doorway that presumably led to the kitchen. Vanessa gathered up the coffee mugs and followed her resignedly.

'How many days is it since you did anything in here?' she enquired as she rolled up her sleeves and set to work on a pile of dishes that spilled out of the sink and on to the draining board.

'Last weekend, I think. And I cleaned the whole place two months ago. It's amazing how quickly the dust accumulates everywhere. Still, a quick flip around with the Hoover and a careful use of subdued lighting will solve that one.' Lydia was blithely unconcerned.

A quarter of an hour later the picture had improved slightly. Piles of clean dishes lay on the kitchen table, the living room was barely presentable if one didn't look too closely and the two girls were busily filling bowls with salads to accompany the assortment of cold meats and quiches that Lydia had bought.

The door bell rang. 'Darn! Someone's early. It

would happen that way round—usually they're all
hours late. Could you be an angel and get that,
Vanessa?'

Vanessa dropped what she was doing and obeyed.
The arrivals were three men whom she didn't know, but
introductions were rapidly made and they came in.
After that a constant stream of people arrived. Clearly
Lydia's reputation as a giver of parties was still as
strong as ever. Vanessa found herself acting as un-
official doorkeeper while Lydia made the finishing
touches to the food and the early arrivals amused themselves. Soon someone had the record-player blaring
away, the lights were arranged dim and inviting, and
the bottles of drink that were arriving with every visitor
were being opened at the makeshift bar at one end of
the room. It was beginning to look considerably more
like a successful party and Vanessa didn't doubt that
things would go with a swing from now on.

The gracious hostess emerged from the kitchen and
greeted people with delighted squeals of recognition and
loving embraces. Vanessa saw a few familiar faces, but
the larger part of the guests was unknown to her. Not
that it mattered. They all seemed a friendly bunch and,
looking the way she did tonight, there was little danger
that she would be left as a wallflower. Lydia's parties
never seemed to suffer from a dearth of unattached men
and she noticed with amusement that the women present were outnumbered by at least three to one.

'Van darling!' Lydia was making signs at her from
the other side of the room. 'Come and meet some of my
friends. I'm getting overwhelmed in this crowd.'

She smiled and was about to comply when the door
bell rang again. 'Hang on, I won't be a second. I'll just
get that.' She went out and opened it, a bright smile on
her face that shattered when she saw who was waiting
impatiently on the doorstep. 'Who invited you?' she

asked rudely, too shaken to disguise her feelings.

'Lydia,' Max said calmly.

'You know Lydia? You never told me.'

'Is there any reason I should have done?' A dark brow registered its owner's frowning disapproval of her impulsive remark. 'As far as I'm aware, I'm not obliged to supply my temporary secretaries with a complete list of my friends and acquaintances. Well, am I allowed in or is the grilling to continue all night?'

Vanessa stood woodenly aside, 'Coats are to the left in the bedroom. The bar is in the living room and the food is——'

'I think I'm just about capable of discovering these things for myself,' he cut her short irritably. 'You can leave me to my own devices.'

'That will be a real pleasure,' she snapped, and stalked off to the kitchen without a backward look. It was bad enough suffering the man in office hours without having to put up with his presence when she was supposed to be enjoying herself. When she emerged from the other room with a plate of food that she didn't really feel like eating, Max was suffering Lydia's clinging embrace with every indication of pleasure.

'Darling,' she cooed. 'So sweet of you to come!'

Vanessa didn't hear his response. She didn't want to. She deliberately made her way over to the other end of the room and started a conversation with a young actor whom she had met briefly at some audition and had found reasonably sympathetic. She resisted the temptation to look round and see what Max was up to. So long as he kept out of her radius, that was fine, she told herself.

Other people drifted over and joined them and Vanessa was soon surrounded by a laughing group, most of whom seemed to be men. Not that she was complaining. When someone asked her to dance, she accepted happily and after that had a succession of partners. After an energetic half hour, she was sitting perched on the end of the sofa idly watching the dancers while she waited for her escort of the moment to return with a drink for her, when a familiar figure loomed into view and eased himself down beside her.

'All alone?' Max asked with a sardonic smile. 'How can that be?'

'I have a partner. He's gone to get me a drink.'

'And here it comes.' Max took the glass from the hand of the younger man, dismissed him with a brief word of thanks and offered it to her. 'What is this concoction?'

'Straight orange, pure and simple,' she said coldly, resenting the way that he had muscled in on her and neatly cut out the opposition.

'You don't need any alcohol to strengthen your reserve tonight? No Sam Galvestons present?'

'No. Everything in the garden's lovely. Or was until a moment ago.'

He ignored the implied insult. 'Do you want to dance?' he asked her.

'Thanks for the kind invitation, but no, thanks.'

'Why not? You've made every man in the room happy, or so it seems. Why turn me down?'

'Do you really think I could make you happy?' she mocked him. 'I wasn't aware I possessed such powers.'

'The age of miracles isn't quite past.'

'I don't mix business and pleasure,' Vanessa told him.

'Neither do I as a general rule.'

'But you're prepared to make an exception in my case? That's very noble of you. But I suffer enough of you during the day. I don't see why I should have to put up with you when I'm trying to enjoy myself.'

'Trying and succeeding, I'd say.'

'Until you came along.'

'You don't mean that and you know it, Vanessa.'

He was right, of course. Where women were concerned Max was usually an accurate observer. She hadn't really been aware of any other man in the room since he arrived. The surface Vanessa had smiled and talked with apparent interest to any number of people and had made the right responses, but the inner Vanessa had been waiting on tenterhooks for just this conversation. Somehow she had known it would come and had half dreaded, half looked forward to it.

'I haven't looked once in your direction since I opened the door to you,' she said in justification.

'No, I'd noticed. But you wanted to, didn't you? And all that determined flirting with every man in the room was intended to tell me something, wasn't it?'

'I come to parties to enjoy myself,' she said, dodging the question.

'Well, let's stop arguing and do just that. Come on, Vanessa.' He was smiling at her persuasively, deliberately charming her. It was a technique that could never have failed him in his relationships with women, that slow, lingering look of appreciation coupled with the suggestion that, for the moment, no other person in the room mattered to him.

He was a handsome devil, she thought irrelevantly, noting how, even in this dim light, the blue of his shirt enhanced the healthy glow of his tanned skin. The tawny eyes were warm as they smiled down at her, compelling her to meet his gaze and sapping her strength to oppose him. She tried to resist the tug of attraction that drew her to him and failed. She let him grasp her hands and draw her to her feet. Almost before she knew it she was on the floor again, responding instinctively to the beat of the music.

'There, that wasn't so bad, was it?' Max asked her wickedly as the record ended.

She shook her head cautiously, scared of admitting how much she had enjoyed the experience. He was a natural dancer, moving lightly on his feet for such a big man and following the rhythm of the music automatically. 'Thank you. That was fun,' she murmured, and prepared to move away, back to a safe corner well away from him as a slow number started.

He prevented her by the simple expedient of taking her hands and tugging her closer to him. She supposed, if she had any sense, she would have resisted him. Perhaps he would have let her go without making an issue of it, although she doubted it somehow. Max wasn't used to being denied what he wanted, she had discovered that much about him, if nothing else. But where he was concerned she had no sense at all. Reason didn't enter into whatever relationship had built up between them. With a sigh Vanessa relaxed in his arms, moulding herself comfortably against the hard contours of his body and abandoning herself to a kind of bliss as they swayed in time to the music.

However much her conscious mind might resent the man, her body had no such inhibitions about him. Her physical senses flared into a vibrant, independent life at his touch and she was no longer capable of controlling the delight she felt when she was near him. She closed her eyes and rested her head on his shoulder, twining her arms around him in shameless abandon and relishing the muscled strength of his broad back as he moved, pressing her against him. The sights and sounds of the party receded into the far distance. Nothing existed except the two of them moving in perfect unison.

He held her lightly, but the touch of his hands burned her through the thin material of her blouse, making her achingly aware of him as she had never been before.

She wondered if she was imagining the softness of his lips on her hair and then as his mouth moved down to plant light kisses on her forehead, knew she had not been mistaken. She raised her head, mutely inviting him to go on, and he claimed her mouth with a sudden hard passion that stirred and excited her.

Vanessa could have stayed in his arms all night, blind and deaf to anything going on around her. And Max wanted her, she could tell that. She was all too aware of the fact that she had awakened a growing need of her in him. But *was* it for her, or would any woman serve in similar circumstances? The question drifted into her mind, but she banished it. He could have had any woman at the party for the snap of his fingers, but he had chosen her. Nothing really mattered anyway but that this half sleeping, half waking ecstasy should go on for ever.

But it seemed that Max had other ideas. She made a small sound of protest as he put her firmly aside and looked up, uncaring that he should see in her eyes the passion that he had aroused in her.

'Max?' She was pleading with him to take her back in his arms.

'We'll get out of this crush, shall we?' It was a question, but he took her assent for granted, leading her to the door. 'Have you got a coat?'

'Yes, I'll get it.' She almost ran to the bedroom, rooted amongst the pile of clothes that littered the bed and retrieved her coat, slipping it over her shoulders as she rejoined him.

'Leaving already?' A cool voice stopped them on the way to the front door.

It was too much to hope that they would get away undetected. Lydia had eyes in the back of her head; she never missed a trick. The avid curiosity in the pale blue eyes that were focussed on them made Vanessa strangely selfconscious about Max's arm draped caressingly around her. What was Lydia going to make of it?

Her disapproval was plain. 'Really, Van, you are the brass-necked limit! You're supposed to be a mate of mine, yet you come to my party and walk off with the most attractive man in the room. I don't call that very friendly!' The words were teasing, but the implication behind them was not.

'Vanessa hasn't any choice in the matter. I'm abducting her.' Max's tone disposed of the matter without further argument. 'Goodbye, Lydia. No doubt we'll see you again.' He didn't sound as if he took much pleasure in the prospect. Perhaps he was annoyed that she should presume to question his actions.

The other girl shrugged and stood aside, saying with faint malice to Vanessa as she did so, 'I see you've changed your tune a bit since we met last.'

'Perhaps.' Vanessa wasn't going to argue the point. She let Max steer her away out into the cool night air. The front door slammed behind them.

CHAPTER EIGHT

'HAVE you eaten? Do you want to?' Max took her arm lightly as they made their way through the garden rubble and found the road again. 'I haven't got the car with me, but we could get a cab somewhere.'

Cabs weren't all that frequent in the darkened streets of Hampstead at this time on a Saturday night, but Vanessa didn't put him to the test. She had no doubt that, if he so desired, a taxi would surface from somewhere within three seconds of his expressing a wish for one.

'I'm not very hungry.' At least, not for food, Vanessa added to herself, and startled herself at the brazenness of the admission. But they hadn't left the crowded party to exchange polite conversation in an equally crowded restaurant, of that she was sure. 'We could go back to my place,' she suggested. 'I could do you something to eat there, if you like?'

'Fine. Let's go.' Max wasn't going to waste any time arguing the point.

Their steps rang out on the pavement, shattering the peace of the quiet streets with the noise. Max's arm was round her, drawing her to him, disturbing her peace with his touch. They did not talk as they headed in the direction of Jill's flat, but it was not an awkward silence. It was rather as if everything of importance was to be postponed until the appropriate place and that the time for trivial small talk was past between them. Suddenly Vanessa felt her heart thumping with an apprehension that held a delicious expectation, like a child at Christmas time.

Her hand shook and she fumbled with the key when they reached the door of the flat at last. He noticed, of course. Would he identify it as reaction to his presence by her side? Somehow it did not matter if he did. He took the key from her without a word and inserted it correctly. The door swung open and Vanessa ushered him inside, feeling a little more secure on home ground as she switched on the lights and took him into the living room.

'Nice.' He strolled casually around the room on a brief tour of inspection, noting the comfortable padded Victorian chairs that were Jill's junk-shop finds, the collection of Toby jugs that was her pride and joy, and the mass of records and books that gave evidence of the two sisters' differing tastes. 'Yours?'

'No. I couldn't afford anything nearly so grand. It's my sister's flat. I'm just sharing it while I'm in London. She was a sitting tenant and had the chance of buying it relatively cheaply. What I pay as rent helps out with the mortgage, but it's still a bit of a struggle for her.' What was she babbling on like this for? Max couldn't be remotely interested.

'She's an actress too?'

'No. She's a secretary. She says one lunatic in the family is quite enough.'

He laughed at that, but not unkindly. 'She's probably right at that. Do I get to meet her?'

'She's away for the weekend.'

'So we've got the place to ourselves.'

'Yes.' Vanessa couldn't read the look he gave her. It held a mixture of devilment and desire and she was not sure which was uppermost. She felt a sudden twinge of panic. Had she done the right thing bringing him here? At the party they seemed to have suddenly found common ground. The antagonism that usually flared between them had vanished, and instead there had been a closeness, an empathy between them. Now she was not so sure.

'What can I get you to eat?' she asked him brightly. 'Coffee and sandwiches? Or would you prefer something else?'

Max had sensed her sudden unease, she could tell by the faint smile that played at his mouth. 'Coffee and sandwiches will do very well for the moment,' he said, the tawny gaze flickering lazily over her. 'You can offer me dessert later.'

What exactly did he mean by *that*? Precisely what she thought he meant, she decided, as her startled eyes caught the wicked glint in his. He was at his old trick of catching her off balance again. She strove to sound unconcerned. 'I won't be long. Make yourself at home, won't you?' She retreated into the kitchen, her heart jumping erratically.

She forced herself to calm down as she automatically sliced and buttered bread and set the percolator in action. She and Jill normally used instant coffee, but Max Anderson couldn't have that. He came into the special guest category. Was that why she was acting like a stupid schoolgirl instead of a grown woman? Her sudden attack of selfconsciousness had amused him, she knew. What had he made of it? The women he usually played around with were in his league. They were aware of the rules of the game and how to bend them to their own purposes. They were sophisticated flirts who knew how to handle this sort of encounter.

But Vanessa wasn't sure of herself whatever Max had assumed to the contrary in the past. There had been men enough in her life who had been keen on her. With her striking good looks it would have been surprising if there had not been. They had all tried their luck with her, but none of them had got very far, simply because she hadn't wanted them to. For the most part they had accepted rejection from her bed with reasonable grace and had stayed friends with her after they had moved on to more accommodating girls. A few had reacted badly, calling her a tease and worse, but these had been rare occasions and, strangely enough, had not upset her too much.

It had occurred to Vanessa sometimes to wonder if the sort of reactions that her friends described at length to her were going to pass her by completely. Now she knew what they were talking about. The jangling nerves, the racing pulse, the weakness in the knees, the general sensation of floating away in a dream world: they were all there in double doses when Max was near her. And, in spite of all her efforts to reject him, she had a shrewd idea that Max knew all too well what effect he had upon her.

Well, one thing was sure, she could not cower in the kitchen all night. She took the tray through, noting that he had followed her invitation to make himself at home. The main light was dark and the softer glow of a table lamp illuminated the room. The gas fire glowed warmly and strains of Debussy came from the record player at one side of the fireplace. If she had been in any doubt as to Max's intentions it was dispelled instantly.

'Mood music?' she asked lightly enough.

'You did tell me to make myself comfortable.'

He'd certainly done that. The dark jacket of his suit had been tossed aside, his tie was loosened and he was lounging full length on the rug by the fire, his back against one of the chairs. He looked a picture of lazy, relaxed ease. She didn't trust him an inch.

She put the coffee tray down at his side and, with that frail barrier between them, sat down herself. 'Help yourself,' she invited him.

He did and ate with good appetite, while she sipped a

cup of coffee and watched him covertly, saying nothing.
Let him make the running. He usually preferred it that
way.

'You're not eating?'

'No. There was food at Lydia's.'

'That's a bloody miracle. I've known her send people
out for Chinese take-aways because she's been too lazy
to cook for them.' A dark brow raised quizzically. 'She
lacks your culinary skills, Vanessa. You'd never do that
to a visitor, would you?'

Was he referring to himself or to Daniel? She ignored
the problem. 'I'm sure Lydia excels in other ways,' she
told him carefully.

'So they tell me.'

She didn't pretend to misunderstand him. Lydia's
reputation was well known to him, presumably. 'You
haven't discovered for yourself?'

'Not for any want of effort on Lydia's part.' His
mouth took on a cynical twist.

'And yet you turned her down?'

'I'm old-fashioned. I prefer to do the chasing myself.
Besides, I don't really fancy being used to further her
career.'

'You've accused me of trying that line more than
once,' she ventured daringly.

'So?'

'What changed your mind?'

'Did I say anything had?' he asked infuriatingly.

'You're sitting here with me,' she pointed out.

'I want to do a little more than just sit with you,
Vanessa. And I think you feel the same way as I do.'
The coffee tray was moved deftly aside with one hand
as the other reached for her and jerked her towards
him. He caught her off guard and she did not resist
him. Afterwards, in the circle of his arms, her head resting against his shoulder, she had no desire to escape.

The spell of his physical presence washed over her, binding her closer to him than any deliberate action on his part could have done. She rested in his arms as if it was the most natural thing in the world for her to do.

His mouth met hers in a passionate demand that made her senses clamour with delight, responding to him with an eagerness that she could not conceal from him. Now that the moment had come she desired him as fervently as he wanted her. There was no holding back. Her probing fingers removed his tie and unfastened the buttons of his shirt, sliding with undisguised delight over the strong, hair-roughened wall of his chest. She felt his hands moving over her, exploring her body with languid assurance as he traced her every curve.

She shivered with pleasure as he lifted her blouse from the waistband of her skirt and caressed the bare skin of her back with a gentleness that tantalised her, before moving to stroke her breasts, stirring them to pulsating life. She made no attempt to dissuade him as he pushed her back to lie on the rug, covering her with his body. The feel of his hard, masculine presence against her brought a new excitement, a growing need of him that she could not have damped down however hard she might have tried. And she didn't want to stop him now.

The pleasurable sensations that were spreading through her were making her lose all control. She responded eagerly as he caressed her, first gently, then with a fever that showed that he was as caught up in the grip of passion as she. His mouth left hers and moved to nuzzle the base of her throat and then the rosy tips of her breasts. A moan of pleasure escaped her as his hands roved more intimately over her, seeking and finding out new sources of delight with every passing second.

She was drowning, lost in a sea of tactile bliss and aware of nothing and no one in the world except the man whose actions were drawing her to the edge of frenzy. She had never allowed a man such freedom with her body, never given herself so wantonly in response. But, with this man, she had no thoughts of holding back. It all seemed so right, so natural. He slipped the flimsy blouse from her shoulders and had tossed it aside and now his hands were seeking the band of her skirt, releasing it and easing it from her. He moved away from her to divest himself of the rest of his clothes and she gave a small sound of protest, impatient at the delay, eager to continue their lovemaking.

'You're beautiful,' he said softly, reaching for her again. Passion flared in his eyes. 'I want you, Vanessa.'

Her hands roamed over the smooth, muscled perfection of him, delighting in the feel of him. Instinct lent knowledge to her inexperience and she could tell from his response that she was pleasing him. She pressed against him, half wanting, half fearing the ultimate excitement, but sure that it would be no disappointment.

And then his hands stilled and he jerked his head away from her, his attention suddenly claimed elsewhere. Her drugged senses registered the fact painfully. She surfaced from her state of mindless content into a jarring world of reality in which the telephone shrilled incessantly.

She shook her head dizzily. 'Shall I answer it?'

Max rolled away from her, making her feel suddenly bereft. 'Up to you,' he said.

She looked at the phone willing it to stop, but it rang on. 'I'd better answer. It might be my sister. She'll worry.'

He shrugged, his face unreadable. The mood was broken. Vanessa sighed as she reached for the receiver. How would one of his sophisticated girl-friends have reacted? Would it have been better to have taken the phone off the hook to prevent interruptions before the evening had got to the interesting stage that it had reached? Or should she just have ignored it? Max had given her no indication of what he wanted her to do.

'Hello?' She noticed that her voice was shaking slightly.

Her caller noticed it too. 'Vanessa? I got you out of bed? I guess I'm making a habit of that. I thought you'd probably be out on the town somewhere on a Saturday night, so I left it late before I rang. I hardly thought you'd be tucked up like a good little girl.'

If only he knew the half of it! 'Daniel, it's you,' she said weakly.

'Who else were you expecting to ring? Trying to make me jealous, are you?' He sounded cheerful as usual.

'No, of course not.' Out of the corner of her eye she saw Max's reaction, an impatient look coming to his face and a hand going out to reach his clothes.

'Hey, are you all right?' Daniel would sense that there was something wrong if she didn't pull herself together and she wasn't sure that she was ready to admit to him that he had interrupted his best friend making passionate love to her.

'Fine. Just tired.' She felt rather than saw the sneer on Max's face.

'Well, I won't keep you.' Daniel sounded disappointed. He'd clearly wanted to talk, one of their usual lengthy chats about nothing in particular and everything under the sun. 'Is Friday still on?'

'Of course it is. I'm looking forward to seeing you.' Concern at the thought of hurting him made Vanessa's voice warmer than it would normally have been, and the response was instant.

'That's great! So am I. For a moment I thought

you'd found someone else.' He was half joking, half serious.

'Would it matter if I had?'

'You bet. Don't fall in love with another guy, will you? I'll tear him apart.'

'I'll bear that in mind, Daniel.'

'Do that thing. I'll see you Friday, then. But I'll ring you before, if that's O.K. with you.'

'That's fine,' she assured him. 'I'm always glad to hear from you.'

They said goodbye and Vanessa rang off. She replaced the receiver and turned to find Max half dressed and shrugging himself into his shirt. 'You're going?' she asked him.

'What does it look like? Do you expect me to stay?'

It was amazing how quickly he could switch from one mood to another. Only minutes ago he had been a passionate, demanding lover, as desperate for her as she had been for him. Now a cold, remote man faced her, a cynical twist to his mouth, contempt and rejection of her in every line of him.

'Is something wrong?' It was a stupid question and she knew it even as she voiced it.

He laughed harshly. 'What do you think?' He finished buttoning his shirt and donned his jacket, shoving his tie in his pocket. 'I must have been mad! I've never taken second place to another man and I don't propose to start now.'

'You mean Daniel?'

'Yes, I mean Daniel. There's no need to play the little innocent with me, so you can wipe that wide-eyed look off your face.'

'I don't know what you're talking about.'

He crossed the room towards her and took her arms in a painful grip. 'Don't you? Do you want me to spell it out to you? I will, if you like.'

'I'm not in love with Daniel,' she protested.

'I'm well aware of *that*. You're not in love with anyone but yourself,' he grated. 'It doesn't matter to you, of course. Out of sight, out of mind. You're quite happy to string him along with sweet nothings over the phone while making sure there's another man around to warm your bed in his place. You little bitch!'

'That's a vile suggestion!'

'But it's true, isn't it? I've had your measure all along.'

'Why did you bother coming back here with me tonight, if you despise me so much?' she challenged him.

'I couldn't help myself,' he said with disgust. 'Does that please you to hear me admit it? I wanted you. I dare say I wanted you as much as you wanted me. And don't try to deny it—you were wild for me. You'd have done anything, wouldn't you?'

She was silent. He was right, of course. But he didn't know that he was the only man who had ever caused her to cast all inhibitions aside and respond in such an abandoned way. And she had no intention of boosting his ego by telling him.

'Tell me one thing, Vanessa. How do I compare with Daniel? Are you as passionate with him? Would any man have done or did your baser feelings get the better of you?' he taunted her.

'You'll never know, will you?'

'Don't worry. I'm not likely to lie awake at night trying to find out an answer.'

'I'm relieved to hear it,' she blazed. 'Now, get out, will you?'

'It'll be a pleasure.' He released her abruptly and strode to the door.

She followed him into the hall. 'Am I to take it that

you'll be finding a new secretary as from Monday morning?'

'No, you're not,' he said curtly. 'You'll be there at nine o'clock or I'll know the reason why. And, Vanessa——' He paused with one hand on the handle of the front door.

'Yes?' she seethed.

'Don't put me to the trouble of coming over to get you. I might lose my temper in the process.'

'Is that a threat?'

'More like a promise. I've had about as much as I can take from you in the last week.'

'The feeling's mutual, believe me.'

He gave a thin smile. 'Then we both know where we stand from now on.'

'Precisely,' she snapped. 'I hate you, Max Anderson!'

'That's a good, honest emotion. It might be the making of you one day. Goodnight, Vanessa.' He opened the door and went through it, not waiting for a response from her.

Vanessa slammed the door shut and locked and bolted it, ramming the bars home with force, as if hurling them at Max's offending head. For the first time she realised that she was naked apart from a pair of brief bikini pants. She had been too angry to be conscious of the fact before. She gave a faint laugh of reaction at the picture she must have made as she bandied words with Max. Not that he had seemed to see anything too incongruous in it. He had been too furious himself to bother about her state of dress—or rather undress.

She wandered back to the living room and picked up her blouse and skirt from the floor where they were lying in an untidy heap. Mechanically she took up the tray with its empty dishes and carried it to the kitchen, dumping it on the draining board. She would deal with it in the morning. Tonight she was too tired. She went to the bathroom and washed, noting as she did so that the angry pressure of his hands had left red marks on her forearms. She would soon be bruised all over, if matters continued the way they had been doing, she thought as she dropped her nightdress over her head and groped her way to her room, stumbling with reaction and weariness.

She put the lights out and lay back, determined to go straight to sleep. She was tired enough by all accounts. She would not think about Max Anderson tonight, not wonder how near he had come to sharing this bed with her until the morning. She would put him entirely from her mind. But the minute she shut her eyes the events of the evening replayed themselves as clearly as if she had deliberately tried to recall them.

She groaned as she attempted and failed to blot out the memory of Max's dark features poised above her, that cynical mouth curved for once in a smile that held no condemnation, but instead something akin to interest in her as a woman. Whatever he had said to her afterwards about despising her, she was sure that, for a brief moment at least, he had cared something for her.

Perhaps she was deluding herself. No doubt hundreds of women had convinced themselves of something similar in the past, only to be cruelly disillusioned. And it was too late now. Daniel's phone call had shattered into a thousand pieces whatever precarious relationship might have been developing. Would Max still have despised her if there had been no interruption and she had let him take her? He would have realised that it was the first time for her. Surely that would have made him rethink his opinion of her? She didn't know what to think any more as she tossed and turned uneasily into the small hours. As the first pale streaks of dawn fil-

tered through the window, she told herself that she
didn't care what Max Anderson did or what opinion he
held of her. There were other men in the world.

But the tears that she cried into her pillow every night
for the following week told a different story. She
dragged herself in to work on Monday morning, believ-
ing Max quite capable of carrying out his threat of
coming to fetch her. She preferred not to put the matter
to the test, although the glint in his eye when he opened
the door to her suggested that he was almost disappointed that he hadn't been given the chance to show
that he meant what he said.

His manner towards her was cool and businesslike.
The perfect employer, in fact. But something else
smouldered beneath the surface, of that she was sure,
and the feeling made her tense and nervous. Each new
day was an effort for her, a strain that ended only when
the door of her bedroom closed behind her at night. She
couldn't bring herself to discuss what had happened
with Jill, and when her sister noted her pale face and
commented on it, she passed it off as overwork.

'I've nearly finished the wretched script and I'm
pushing myself to get it done.' It wasn't a lie. The
sooner that she typed the last line of the play the sooner
she could get away from Max.

'Is he bothering you about it, getting impatient?'

'No.' Strangely enough, he wasn't. It was almost as
if Max was enjoying the game he was playing with her,
constantly nerving her for some kind of confrontation
that never came. She would have thought he would
have been as glad to see the back of her as she would be
to go. 'I just want to move on, that's all.'

'You're a restless creature, Van. I take it there's
still no love lost between you?'

'None at all,' she agreed a shade too quickly, and Jill
gave her a sudden suspicious look.

'You haven't fallen for him, have you, Van?'

'Of course not,' she snapped back. 'Don't be ridiculous!' But she had a feeling that Jill wasn't entirely convinced, for all that she said nothing further on the subject.

When Daniel saw her he was less easily diverted. 'What's happened to you? Have you been ill?' was his first reaction when he arrived at the flat to pick her up for their date and saw her white face and the shadows under her eyes that she had tried and failed to conceal with make-up.

'I'm fine,' she lied defensively.

'Well, you sure don't look like it to me.'

'That's a great thing to say to a girl when she's spent an age getting herself ready for you!' She pretended indignation at his words, hoping to distract him. 'And I bought a brand new dress just for you.'

He laughed. 'I came to see you, not your dress.'

'Do you like it?' she persisted, twirling round to show off the fullness of its flared red skirt which contrasted well with the tightly fitting bodice. She had bought it in a Hampstead boutique in a mad attempt to cheer herself up, telling herself that, if Max was always going to see her as a scarlet woman, she might as well start dressing the part. Not that Max would ever see her in it. The thought depressed her, she didn't know why.

Daniel smiled and said all the right things. But he was not an easy man to fob off, she discovered, when he wanted information about something. He drove her out to the restaurant of his choice, a small place just outside Richmond with a garden that went down to the Thames, and waited until they were comfortably seated and had chosen their meal before returning to the topic.

'Vanessa?'

'What?' She looked up at him and smiled.

'You look like an ad for a nerve tonic. Before, not after,' he told her bluntly. 'What's wrong?'

'You're like a dog with a bone, Daniel. I've already said that there's nothing at all wrong with me.' She refused to meet his eyes, studying the tablecloth as if it fascinated her.

'You're not the same girl I took out last time I was over.'

'Sorry.' She tried to sound flippant and failed dismally.

'So it's Max. I thought it might be.'

'I don't want to talk about him. I hate the man!'

Daniel gave a lopsided grin. 'I wish I'd a dollar for every time I've heard a woman say that about Max. They never mean it, of couse.'

'I do,' she claimed stubbornly.

'Max isn't the most trusting of men,' Daniel said carefully. 'When he decides that he likes you, there's nothing he won't do for you. I know that from past experience. But it takes a while.'

'I could try until doomsday and he won't change his mind about me, I'm sure.'

'Do you want him to? Is it that important to you?' he asked.

'Yes, it is.' The answer came automatically and surprised her with its force of feeling. For days now she had been telling herself that Max Anderson was insufferable, arrogant, conceited and heartless and that she didn't care a rap about him.

'You're in love with him.' Daniel stated it even as she realised the truth herself.

'I'm sorry,' said Vanessa.

'Sorry it's not me you fell for? So am I.' He gave her a rueful look. 'Because I like you, Vanessa. I like you a lot. We've not spent a lot of time together, but what we have had has been fun. You're the first girl in a long time that I've really enjoyed myself with.'

'I like you too, Daniel.' She was touched by his obvious sincerity. 'But——'

'But it's Max.'

'Yes.' She pulled herself together and gave him a shaky smile. 'Don't worry, I'll get over it. All the others do, don't they?'

'Perhaps.' He sounded non-committal.

Max was a friend of his. She had no right to be discussing it with him. 'I'm sorry, I shouldn't have said anything. It's not fair on you.'

'I dragged it out of you. You didn't want to tell me. I wish there was something I could do to help.'

'Nice of you to volunteer, Daniel, but I doubt if anyone could disentangle the mess,' she said wearily. 'I don't understand him at all, and he claims to understand me all too well.'

Daniel drummed his fingers against the table top and appeared to come to a decision. 'Look, I don't know what's gone wrong between you and I don't want to know the ins and outs of it. I only know that every time he's caught me with you Max has looked as if he'd like to wring my neck.'

'Or mine,' Vanessa told him dismally.

'He doesn't usually give a damn about that sort of thing. In fact, in the past, I've taken quite a few girls off his hands when he got tired of——'

'Being adored by them?'

'Something like that,' Daniel admitted. 'But he doesn't show any signs of doing it with you. I only wish he would.'

'I'm not a parcel to be passed on, you know. I have got a mind of my own.'

'Not a very good one, if you prefer Max to me,' he

teased her, then sobered again. 'We've been friends a long time, the two of us. It must be ten years now since I first met him.'

'Over here?'

'No. He was in New York on an assignment for his paper. I was just making a name for myself in the world of finance. He thought I might make a good article on up and coming talent.' He smiled at the memory. 'Max didn't suffer fools gladly even then. And neither did I. We had a good deal in common.'

'What was he like then?' Vanessa asked.

'Not much different than he is today, except that he hadn't got to the top yet. He was heading there, though. It took him another five years before he really made it, but the talent was always there. Everyone recognised it.'

'Especially women, I suppose.'

'Then as now,' Daniel agreed. 'But Max wasn't interested. He had a girl back home that he was crazy about. She was an actress, and was going to marry her. He carried her picture in his wallet, talked about her all the time. She was waiting for him, he said.'

'What happened?' Vanessa tried and failed to imagine a younger, softer Max, madly in love with someone. It wasn't a picture that fitted the hard, cynical man she knew who used women like playthings.

'She threw him over,' Daniel said briefly. 'He went back to London when he was through in New York. He had the ring in his pocket to put on her finger. He'd even conned me into flying over to be his best man at the ceremony. And when he got back he found that she'd dropped him to go and live with a guy who could offer her more—money and jobwise.'

A lot of things about Max's attitude to women were suddenly becoming explicable. 'He must have hated her,' Vanessa said slowly.

'I don't know about that. But she made a fool of him

and that he couldn't take. He's a proud man. He's taken good care never to let a woman get to him like that again.'

She stretched a hand across the table towards him. 'Thank you for telling me, Daniel. I appreciate it.'

He laughed. 'I don't know why I'm sitting here helping you mope over another man. I should be doing my best to further my own interests. Where's that waiter gone? I think they've forgotten us.'

It was a signal to her that he had said all he intended to say about his friend, and Vanessa respected it. He had given her a valuable insight into the character of the man she loved and he was leaving matters there. It was for her to take them further, if she wanted.

But would it make a scrap of difference to Max what she did? Somehow Vanessa doubted it.

CHAPTER NINE

SHE had many more outings with Daniel in the course of the next few days. He had decided, he told her, to base himself in England for a week or two. Vanessa was not foolish enough to assume that it was on her account, obviously business dictated the move, but he made it all too clear that he enjoyed her company and wanted to spend his free time with her.

And she was happy to oblige him. They had a lot in common, she discovered. Their tastes in music and films coincided. They both liked walking in the rain and spending hours in second-hand bookshops. They could spend an afternoon in an art gallery and then go on dancing half the night. Both preferred the country to the town, although in each case work forced them away from their chosen environment except at the weekends. They liked travelling, although Daniel had seen far more of the world than Vanessa had been able to do. And she was the first girl he had taken out, he declared, who understood his zany sense of humour.

'In fact, you're a girl in a million,' he told her at the end of one particularly enjoyable evening, catching her to him and kissing her lightly. She did not repulse him. He had not made any sexual play for her, deliberately holding off, as if sensing that she would not welcome a move in that direction, and she was grateful to him for his understanding. She liked Daniel as a friend and good-natured companion, but anything more was definitely out until she came to her senses over Max. And there were times when she thought that would never happen.

Common sense told her that she would get over him. Love didn't last for ever except in story books. In time the raw hurt that her emotions were causing her would fade and she would be happy with someone else. This was just a passing phase, she assured herself doggedly. But every time she looked up from her work at Max's tall, powerful figure across the room, her heart turned over and she forced her eyes back to the typewriter, terrified that he might read the naked feeling for him that her expression contained. She was sure that it would only amuse him.

Not that much seemed to be diverting him these days. He was brisk and businesslike with her, his face a cool, impassive mask that never revealed his thoughts to her. By tacit consent what communication there was between them was brief and to the point. Max wasted no time on being pleasant to her and personal matters were never discussed. She could have been a piece of the furniture, she thought resentfully, for all the interest he took in her as a woman. Sometimes she wondered if she had dreamed the passionately demanding lover that he had been that night in Jill's flat. It was as if what had been between them was past and forgotten, an interlude thrust aside by him as if it was of no consequence.

Presumably to him it was exactly that, a trifling interlude to be dismissed from his mind. He wasn't a man to waste time wondering about what might have been. Unlike Vanessa, who spent hours in fruitless asking herself what she could have done differently in order to keep him with her that fateful night when Daniel's phone call had ruined everything between them. They had been on the edge of an understanding, that time, she was sure. That had been her chance to convince him of what the real Vanessa Herbert was like. And she had thrown it away the second she had picked up the phone.

It was useless to try to explain that there was nothing between herself and Daniel. Max could hardly fail to be aware that she was seeing his friend. Daniel was a well known figure and his romantic life was always good for a few paragraphs in the press. The gossip columnists had seized upon his new girl-friend with interest and photographs of the two of them dining out together had already appeared, accompanied by sly suggestions as to where Daniel's interest in her might be leading.

She didn't like it and told Daniel so. 'My private life is private and I'd rather it stayed that way.'

He shrugged, pushing back the untidy mop of blond hair that would persist in falling in his eyes despite all his efforts. 'Sorry, Van, there's not that much I can do about it. If I have a word and tell them to lay off, they'll only get more interested. Likewise if we try to shake them off. It's best just to ignore them and hope they'll get tired of us. There'll be some new story to-morrow, you'll see.'

'Meanwhile, I'd better learn how to eat spaghetti elegantly for the camera in future,' she said ruefully, looking at a particularly candid shot of her that had appeared.

'The penalties of fame,' Daniel warned her. 'Wait until you're a successful actress. I warn you, Vanessa, you'll be ringing up to complain when you don't feature in the gossip columns.'

'Never,' she assured him vehemently. 'I shall be like Garbo and guard my privacy jealously.'

They laughed over it and Vanessa stopped worrying. But the rumours persisted. 'When are the wedding in-vitations going out?' Max asked her abruptly one morn-ing as he leafed through one of the papers.

It was the first purely personal remark that he had made to her for ages and she looked at him in surprise. 'What do you mean?' she asked warily.

'Isn't it immediately obvious to you?' He took up the paper again and read, 'Wedding bells for Daniel Jensen? It seems the footloose financier has been grounded at last. Lucky recipient of his million-dollar favours is actress Vanessa Herbert. Yesterday the couple had no comment to make about their future plans, but Daniel agreed that they were very happy together. Watch this space for future developments.' He made a sound of disgust and tossed the offending piece aside as if it sickened him. 'Well?'

'Don't believe everything you read in the papers,' she said carelessly. 'I'd have thought that you of all people would realise that.'

'So it's not serious?'

'Does it matter to you whether it is or not?' Vanessa was curious.

'Daniel hasn't said anything to me.'

'Were you expecting him to? Does he usually discuss his girl-friends with you?'

'Sometimes.' He frowned at her. 'He's keeping remarkably quiet about you at the moment.'

She managed an amused laugh. 'Are we worrying you, Max?'

'Not at all,' he said. 'Are you going to marry him?'

'He hasn't asked me—yet.'

'And when he does?'

'That's my business,' she told him coolly.

She expected him to leave it at that, but he didn't. 'Are you in love with him?'

'You surely don't expect me to answer that question?' She was fencing with him now, deliberately dodging the issue. He had no right to question her like this. But where Max was concerned rights didn't come into it. He expected her to supply him with the answers because it suited him, whatever reservations she might have about doing so. Well, for once he was going to be disappointed!

'No, you're not in love with him, are you? Exactly what game are you playing, Vanessa? Are you hoping he'll marry you so you can heave a sigh of relief and abandon that so-called career as an actress?' There was a harsh, taunting note in his voice as he fired the questions at her.

She wasn't going to lose her temper with him, she told herself. But it was an effort. 'Perhaps,' she said calmly. 'Who knows?'

He looked as if he would like to shake her. His hands clenched into two fists as if he was having trouble keeping them off her. 'You mean if someone better comes along you'll drop Daniel like a hot brick. But, in the meantime, being seen out on the town with him is doing you no harm at all.'

She shrugged. 'If that's what you like to think,' she said.

'It's the truth, isn't it?'

'I don't have to justify myself to you, Max, and I don't intend to. My private life is my affair.'

'Don't come running to me when it all blows up in your face, that's all,' he snarled.

'You're the last man on earth I'd run to under any circumstances,' she said emphatically.

He slammed out of the room without deigning to reply and Vanessa turned back to her work again. In any other man but Max she would assume that all those questions about her relationship with Daniel betokened jealousy. But Max Anderson didn't care enough about her to harbour such an emotion. He didn't care about anybody except his arrogant self. And yet she couldn't stop herself loving him. What kind of masochist was she to suffer the pain that he inflicted on her and come back for more?

She said as much to Daniel. 'I'm a fool. I don't know why you waste your time with me.'

'I like you,' he told her simply. 'I could do more than like you, if you'd let me, Vanessa.'

She made a stifled sound of protest. 'No. It's no use.'

He took her hand. 'Not now. Not yet, perhaps. But later, when you've got over Max.'

Vanessa shook her head. 'No. It wouldn't be fair to ask you to hang around on that kind of basis. I like you as a friend, but that's it. I ought to love you, you know.' She smiled at him. 'Goodness knows, most women would grab at the chance. You're attractive, intelligent, good-humoured, kind, understanding——'

'Don't go on,' he said hastily. 'You make me sound like a parcel of virtues. Too boring for words!'

'Oh, you've got your faults. Haven't we all?'

He laughed. 'You needn't catalogue those. I think I know them by now.' His face was serious again. 'I'm not going to stop seeing you, Vanessa. Don't ask me to do that.'

She hesitated. 'All right, I won't. But——'

'I know. I won't push my luck. And, Vanessa——'

'Yes?'

'I'm always around if you need help. Remember that, will you?'

'Thank you.' She was grateful to him for taking the line he had. She knew that she would miss his cheerful, undemanding company if it was suddenly taken away from her. At the moment she needed something or someone to take her mind off her troubles.

She threw herself into work and finally completed the play script. It seemed to have taken years to finish, but that was Max's fault. He had expected her to cope with a mass of day-to-day secretarial work as well and had been constantly amending and re-writing pages that she had typed. It had been a back-breaking job and she had become heartily sick of it, but at last it was done. She looked at the slim blue folder that contained the neatly typed work with some satisfaction. Job specification completed, there was nothing to keep her here any longer. She was free to go and, away from Max's disturbing presence, make some attempt to put him from her mind.

'It's done,' she told him, when he entered the living room, half an hour after she had completed the task and was engaged in tidying up some routine details of correspondence.

He walked over to the desk, opened the folder and studied the last few pages carefully. Vanessa waited. She wasn't worried that he would find errors. She had checked and double checked and she knew they had been typed immaculately. Her eyes lingered automatically on him, admiring the strength in the long brown fingers that held the papers. She could never look at his hands without recalling how they had stroked and caressed her to a state of mindless rapture. Would any other man ever have the same effect upon her? She doubted it somehow. But it was a foolish daydream of hers to hope that Max would ever want to make love to her again.

'Yes, that's all right.' He jammed the pages back in the folder and slung it back on the desk, turning to look at her as he did so.

She didn't know what reaction she had expected from him. Praise at a job well done, she supposed. Well, it was evident that none was forthcoming. 'So I can go now,' she said cautiously.

'If you want to.'

'I thought you'd be glad to see the last of me.'

'You've certainly caused me more upset than the average secretary I've employed,' he agreed. There was a pause. 'My other girl isn't coming back.'

'So?' Did he mean he wanted her to stay on?

'You could continue working here, if you liked. Your typing's not bad and you've dealt with everything else reasonably well. In time you could be quite useful to me.' His voice was level, containing no hint of expression.

'Could I?' Vanessa asked. 'How very kind of you to say so.' For one wild moment she thought of swallowing her pride and accepting his offer, however ungraciously it had been made. But then reason reasserted itself. There was no point dragging herself here every day, hoping against hope that one day Max would suddenly reform his opinion of her. Better to cut loose completely, however painful she found it. There was no point in waiting for a miracle to happen.

'So what's your answer?'

For one self-deceiving moment Vanessa almost fooled herself into thinking he sounded interested in her reply. Then she pulled herself together and told herself she was mistaken. 'No, thank you,' she said coldly.

'It's a genuine offer. A permanent job.'

'I don't want it, thanks.'

'I don't suppose you've got anything better lined up, have you?' he asked.

'That's not your problem,' she told him calmly. 'I'll manage somehow.'

'If you turn it down, that's the end of the matter as far as I'm concerned. Don't think the job will be waiting for you still when you change your mind and come and ask for it again.'

'I wouldn't dream of doing any such thing.' She raised her chin defiantly. 'I've had enough of this place *and* its owner to last me a lifetime!'

There was a white, tense look about Max's mouth as if he was struggling to keep his temper in check and finding it a hard task. 'You don't mince words, do you?'

'Did you expect me to?' she flared.

'No, not really. But if you're in the mood for a spot of plain speaking you can answer me this. Are you going to move in with Daniel? Is he going to be your meal ticket from now on?'

'It's nothing to do with you. It's not your concern what I do with my life.'

'I'm making it my concern,' he said grimly. He seized hold of her and gave her an impatient shake. 'Are you going to Daniel?'

'Find out!' she spat defiantly, struggling in vain to escape arms that held her fast to him, immovable as steel bands.

'I fully intend to, one way or another. And, as I remember, you've always responded to my methods of persuasion in the past.' There was devilment in the face that was so close to hers. She knew that if he kissed her she was lost for all time.

'All right,' she capitulated. 'If you really want to know, I don't see it matters one bit. Yes, I'm going to Daniel.'

'You scheming little bitch,' he said softly.

She didn't know why she had lied to him. She would sooner fly to the moon than land herself on Daniel, although she had no doubt at all that he would be only too delighted if she did so. She supposed that, in a strange kind of way, she was trying to live up to the blackened picture that Max had drawn of her activities. Let him think the worst of her! She didn't care any more so long as she never had to set eyes on him again. And, by the look of his face, pale with anger, she had achieved that aim.

'I make the most of the chances that come my way,' she said with assumed carelessness. It was the sort of remark that she had heard Lydia make many times by way of self-justification, but she had never expected to use it on her own account.

'And so do I,' he replied harshly as his mouth bent to claim hers with sudden intensity.

Vanessa despised herself for responding, but she couldn't damp down the fires of desire that sprang to ready life as Max made her mouth his own. He was taking her in anger, but she didn't care, didn't think of anything beyond the shattering sensations that his kiss was arousing. Nothing mattered except the pounding in her head, the excitement rising within her, the need to be his and his entirely.

When he released her he was smiling, but it was a smile of cold satisfaction. He knew what he did to her, the effect his body had on hers, and that kiss had been a calculated breach of her defences. He had wanted to reduce her to a trembling mass of emotion and he had done so quite deliberately.

'Does Daniel kiss you like that?' he asked her.

'I won't tell you.'

'You don't need to,' he said cruelly. 'Your body answered for you. Whatever it is you're craving for, Daniel isn't satisfying you.'

'And you can, I suppose?'

'Haven't I just proved it to you? Do you want me to demonstrate again?'

'No,' she said hastily, turning her face away from him. She couldn't take any more without breaking down completely.

'I thought not.' He sounded contemptuous. 'You're rather a coward when it comes to facing facts about yourself, aren't you?'

Only where he was concerned, she thought, but didn't

say so out loud. 'When do you want me to leave?' she asked instead.

He looked indifferent. 'You can go now, if you like. I don't give a damn.'

He wouldn't. 'But it's only eleven o'clock,' she protested.

'Oh, I'll pay you until the end of the day, if that's what's worrying you.'

'But isn't there anything else I could be——'

'There's nothing here for you,' he said, and words summed up everything that she felt about him. It was hopeless even to care any more. Max Anderson wasn't for her. He never had been.

She tidied up her things in silence while he watched her broodingly. There wasn't much to take away with her—a couple of pens, a few bits of make-up from the desk drawer, a box of tissues. She packed them in her bag, blinking back the tears of reaction to his cruel words that were already starting to her eyes. She wouldn't give him the satisfaction of seeing that he had hurt her, she vowed.

'Well, that seems to be everything.' He could see that for himself, but she said it anyway in a falsely bright voice. 'I'll be going, then, if you're quite sure that——'

'Quite sure,' he said firmly. 'Goodbye, Vanessa.'

She managed a strangled sound that approximated to 'goodbye' and almost ran from the room, despite her intent to remain cool and calm. In the lift to the ground floor the tears that she had held back streamed unchecked. She scrubbed furiously at her cheeks with her handkerchief as she walked to the bus stop, conscious that she was attracting the attention of passers by.

When Jill got home that evening she greeted her suspiciously red around the eyes, but determinedly cheerful, and with news to give her that, in her sister's view at least, took precedence over the reason for the parting of the ways with Max Anderson and postponed questions on that score.

'Jonathan rang me. It's strange how it works out sometimes. No news of any work for ages and now, according to him, the chance of the century, if I do all right at the audition tomorrow.'

Jill pulled a face. 'Don't build up too many hopes, love. Remember what happened last time.'

'I know. But this one's different, he says. A better chance for me and a nice meaty part. Anyway, whatever happens, it's work again, or the possibility of it. I'd almost forgotten what a stage looked like. And if I'm lucky and get the part there'll be a six-week tour of the provinces before we hit London. Plenty of time to work myself into the role and get over my nerves.'

'Just see that you get it, that's all,' her sister cautioned.

'Wet blanket!' Vanessa accused her, and Jill laughed. 'Have you told Daniel the good news yet?'

'Yes. We were due to go out tonight, but now I'll have to stay in and go over some likely audition pieces.' Vanessa smiled, remembering his enthusiastic response. 'I think he was more thrilled than I was about it all.'

It was strange really. Only a short while ago she would have been over the moon at the prospect of a second chance to show that she had talent and to work in the theatre that she loved so much. Once it would have been all she had asked from life. But now she knew that there was so much more that she wanted. Her single-minded passion for work had waned, diluted by an equal feeling for a man who cared nothing for her.

As she set off for the audition next morning Vanessa was resolved on one point at least. She was going to do her level best to get the part. And, if she got it, she would work as hard as was humanly possible to perfect it. She would show Max Anderson that, for once, one of his forcefully expressed opinions was wrong. She would make him eat his words about her acting talents.

She was nervous, naturally, but she did her best, hoping it would be good enough. The part that she was being considered for seemed tailor-made for her in her present state, she thought. It was that of a young girl gripped by an obsessive love for a man who cared nothing for her. Her descent from reality into a terrifying world of shadows and delusions was brilliantly written. It was a gem of a part, Vanessa realised from her brief glimpse of the script, and she ached to play it.

Like the other actresses present she gave the speech that she had prepared for the occasion and then attempted a short scene from the play that had been picked out as a test for them. She was given ten minutes to study it, not nearly enough by any standards, and was then summoned on stage to run through it, the stage manager, a young, casually dressed man in his early thirties, reading the other part in the piece, that of the man the young girl loved.

Vanessa had heard him with the others who had gone before her. He read the lines clearly enough, but, after playing the scene through with nine different girls, he was beginning to get bored and he sounded it. He looked at his watch as she walked on to the stage and called down to the stalls, 'How many more to get through? Is this the last one?' as if she didn't exist.

She'd make him sit up and take notice! Vanessa decided angrily, her nerves suddenly vanishing in a wave of indignation. Just who did he think he was? She launched into her first speech with a confidence born of blind fury.

She was allowed to go to the end of the scene. Nobody stopped her halfway with the brief 'Thank you' that had been the fate of some of the others. When she

finished she sensed a buzz of excitement in the dim
blackness beyond the stage. She was sure she had done
well even before the stage manager came over to congratulate her on her reading. His bored tone had
vanished after the first few seconds and he acted the
piece for all he was worth, giving her all the help and
encouragement that he could.

'You were great,' he said, coming over to where she
stood, exhausted by the nervous effort that the last few
moments had entailed. 'You've got the part.'

She managed a grin at him, her anger suddenly eva-
porating. 'And how long have the powers-that-be been
listening to you when it comes to hiring and firing
people?'

He laughed. 'They'll agree with me, you'll see.'

And he was proved right. She was asked to wait, but
after only a few more minutes she was told the part was
hers. The man who was to direct the play came over to
give her the news. 'We'll be in touch with your agent
about the details of salary, etc. Rehearsals start next
week. See you then.'

Vanessa floated out of the theatre on wings, barely
touching the pavement in her excitement. She rang
Jonathan with the good news, then got in touch with
Jill and Daniel. For half a second she was tempted to
ring Max and tell him. She had a childish desire to
prove to him that, even if he thought she was a lousy
actress, other people had thought differently. But that
would hardly change his opinion of her. Max Anderson
didn't care what other people thought. He was so sure
he was always right. He would only receive her news
with some cutting remark that would upset her, however much she tried to ignore it. Let him read about it
all in the papers, she decided. He could make what he
liked about the news.

She celebrated, of course. Daniel brought champagne

round to the flat that evening and the three of them toasted her success. Daniel took her out for dinner afterwards and she laughed and talked with him as if she hadn't a care in the world. She *was* happy about the play. It was a chance in a million and she had pulled it off. And Daniel was fun to be with. But somehow her thoughts would persist in returning to the cold, hard look on Max's face when he had said goodbye to her the previous day.

Why couldn't she put him from her mind as easily as he had no doubt dismissed her? He wouldn't be wasting his time the way she was. Every time a tall, broad-shouldered man with Max's dark colouring entered the restaurant she caught herself craning forward, only half her attention on what Daniel was saying to her, until she had established that it was not Max.

'Darling, you're not listening to a word I'm saying.' She came back to earth with a bump and heard Daniel reproaching her.

'Sorry,' she said guiltily. 'I was just thinking——'

'Dreaming of your name in lights?' he teased. 'Will you still talk to me when you're famous?'

'You're a fool, Daniel.' She laughed and for the rest of the evening made a conscientious effort to stop her thoughts from straying again.

'He's a nice man,' Jill commented when he delivered Vanessa back to the flat at a reasonable hour, chatted over a cup of coffee with the two of them and then took his leave politely.

'Daniel?'

'Who did you think I meant?'

Certainly not Max Anderson. No one in their right mind would describe him as anything of the sort. 'Yes, Daniel is nice,' Vanessa agreed.

'Will you marry him when he asks you?'

'He hasn't asked me.' She'd been through this catechism before with a sharper questioner than Jill. Vanessa closed her eyes at the sudden pain of the memory.

'He will do. He's crazy about you, Van. Anyone with half an eye can see that.'

'Maybe.' She wasn't interested in proposals from Daniel. She wondered how she would react if it was Max asking her to marry him, his face full of love for her, anxiously waiting for her answer. She smiled at the thought. Max wasn't the sort of man to ask a woman anything. He would tell her with all his usual arrogance and that would be an end of it. The woman on whom his choice finally settled would be lucky if he consulted her in any detail. But somehow she had a feeling that Max's bride-to-be—if he ever got round to selecting one—wouldn't mind too much about that. Vanessa certainly wouldn't.

But it was no use daydreaming. That was the road to disaster. It wasn't going to be her floating down the aisle with Max Anderson; she had better accept it. Thoughts of him were too distracting. Work was the thing, she told herself, and threw herself into the business of reading her script when it arrived, analysing the character that she was playing and trying to think herself into the part.

And the therapy worked to a certain extent. Soon she was caught up in rehearsals, travelling to a dreary little church hall in Kilburn, which always managed to be freezing cold despite the central heating turned on at full blast. It was a small cast, but they were a pleasant bunch and she had no problems in working with them. What with costume fittings, extra rehearsals, new lines to be learnt when the author, who was on hand throughout, had another flash of inspiration, Vanessa's days were crowded. In the evenings, when she finally got home, she was usually too dead on her feet to do more than make herself something to eat before crawling into bed exhausted.

She had never worked so hard in her life. Daniel moaned that he was seeing nothing of her these days and although she tried to placate him with promises of making it up to him at a later date, she wasn't at all sure that it was a bad thing that she was so busy. She didn't want to overencourage Daniel. She liked him too much to offer him only second-rate feeling. She couldn't ever love him, she knew that now, and she supposed that at some time in the future she would have to break the fact to him and stop him hoping. He knew how she felt about Max. He was the only person who did, although Vanessa sensed by her very silence on the subject that Jill had guessed a good deal. But he was waiting around for a miracle that wasn't going to happen, loving her as impossibly as she loved Max.

She hadn't seen sight or sound of Max since the day she had left his flat, but she braced herself daily for the time when they would inevitably meet. The theatre world, particularly in London, was a small one and there was no possibility of avoiding him for ever. When it was announced that there would be a small reception for the press before the play went on its provincial tour, Vanessa's heart sank. He was bound to be there. No one gave that kind of gathering without inviting the most influential spokesman on the arts, the man whose encouragement could make or break the play. Max Anderson was bound to be on the guest list.

She toyed with the wild idea of feigning illness instead of turning up, then rejected it. If Max got to hear of it he would only assume, and rightly so, that she was too much of a coward to face him. Instead she took particular pains with her face and hair, put on the new dress that she had bought specially for the occasion, a

Mexican smock in virginal white, brilliantly embroidered with butterflies around the hem, and, with a drink in her hand, waited with the rest of the cast for their guests to arrive.

The reception was being held in one of the conference suites of a West End hotel. It was not an over-large room and the place soon began to fill up. Vanessa's heart stopped jumping every time the door opened to admit a new arrival. If he did come she would see and be able to dodge him in this crush. The introductions had already made the cast known to those who had arrived on time and now they were circulating through the room, answering questions about themselves and the play and generally doing their best to promote the production. A good press mention before they opened in London could make quite a difference to the state of advance bookings.

Out of the corner of her eye Vanessa saw a dark head that looked familiar, but then its owner turned and she breathed a sigh of relief when she realised that she was mistaken. As the minutes ticked by she began to relax more. An hour had gone by now. It was clear that, although he must surely have been invited, Max hadn't chosen to favour them with his presence. Perhaps he had more interesting things to do. He had probably sent a deputy in his place. Had he known that she would be there? He might have decided that he couldn't face the thought of being polite to her in company.

Then a voice from behind her greeted her coolly. 'Vanessa—this is a surprise!'

She turned to face him, leaving the man she was talking to in mid-sentence. 'Max.' Her voice was a little high-pitched with nerves, but otherwise she was in control of herself and felt quite proud of the fact. 'Why a surprise?' she asked. 'I am in the play. Or didn't you know?'

He was looking every inch the successful man of the world. The other journalists present sported a variety of casual attire from scruffy jeans to shabby suits that had seen better days. A few were presentable, some were even fashionable. But no man there could hold a candle to Max Anderson. He was wearing an immaculately cut navy suit, teamed with crisp white linen that emphasised the healthy tan of his face. Why did he always have to look as if he was just back from three months on some Caribbean beach? Vanessa thought resentfully. His dark hair was combed ruthlessly back. He'd had it cut since she saw him last, she noted absently. She remembered its springy, healthy feel against her hands the last time she had kissed him. Did he remember too?

It seemed he wasn't in the mood for nostalgic memories. 'Yes,' he said in answer to her question, 'I knew you'd landed the plum part in this production. But somehow I didn't think that even you would have the nerve to face me with the fact.'

'Why on earth not? Do you really think that actresses you condemn should have the good sense never to tread a stage again?'

'No.' His face was a hard mask of disapproval. 'But I do expect them to get parts on merit.'

'What do you mean?'

'Don't try to con me—it won't work. Daniel's backing the production. Are you expecting me to believe that he didn't buy you the part? You'd better be good, Vanessa, I'm warning you. Because, if you're not, I'll crucify you when I review the play. I'll see you never have the chance to act again—anywhere!'

And, having said what he felt, he turned away and left her standing, white-faced, in the middle of the crowded room.

CHAPTER TEN

Vanessa tackled Daniel as soon as she could get hold of him, taking the bold step of going directly to the London offices of his firm and bulldozing her way through all the attempts of secretaries and personal assistants to put her off. When, after a great deal of argument and hassle, she was finally ushered into his private sanctum, she felt more like bursting into tears than anything else.

Daniel sensed her distress, coming forward to greet her and taking her comfortingly in his arms. 'Hey, nothing's that bad, is it?' He led her to a comfortable sofa in one corner of the room and sat her down on it. She heard him issuing orders for coffee to be brought to them and when it arrived he gave instructions that they were not to be disturbed. He poured her a cup and one for himself and sat down beside her. 'Well, Van, what's wrong?'

She pulled herself together and explained what had happened. 'Is it true?' she asked desperately. 'Did you get me the part?'

'No,' he said, but he refused to meet her eyes. Instead he stirred his coffee as if his life depended upon it.

'You're lying!' she accused him. She got to her feet and made for the door.

'Where are you going?'

'To give up the part. I've never got anything in a dishonest way and I don't intend to start now. I know you did it for the best, Daniel. I'm not blaming you in any way. Just accept that I can't take that kind of help, however well you meant it.'

He strode towards her and took hold of her. 'Listen, Van, for a moment, will you? You've got it all wrong.'

'I can't see how. You've as good as admitted that you pulled strings. I can see the guilt in your face. You don't have to say anything.'

'I do,' he said firmly. 'Sit down and listen to me. I'll explain. If you still want to leave the cast when I've told you about my part in it all, I won't stand in your way.'

She subsided reluctantly to the sofa again. 'I've made up my mind. But go on.'

He shrugged helplessly. 'I'm interested in the theatre. I always have been. And I'm a wealthy man, wealthy enough to indulge my whims sometimes and back productions that I think have a fair chance of getting somewhere. I don't often lose money on the deal.'

'And I'm one of your whims?' she asked him bitterly.

'The money was put up for your play long before I got to know you. Believe me, Vanessa.'

She shrugged. 'All right, I believe you so far. Where do I come into it?'

He gave an impatient sigh. 'I met you. I liked you a lot. I wanted to help you.'

'I know. You told me you could pull a few strings. But I didn't want that kind of help—I told you that, Daniel.'

'I didn't do that much. They'd already shortlisted a few actresses for the main part. I knew they were having problems finding someone, so I pulled rank and asked them to audition you. And that was all. The rest was up to you. I'm telling you the truth, Van. If you're sensible you'll believe it. There's no way I would expect them to cast you in the lead if you weren't up to it. You electrified them at the audition. Someone told me afterwards that it was like the answer to a prayer. You were exactly what they were looking for.'

'So I did get it on merit,' Vanessa said slowly.

'Of course you did. I just ensured that you had the chance to be considered.'

'Why didn't you tell me?'

Daniel looked faintly embarrassed. 'I wasn't sure if you would approve. And, even if you didn't mind, I didn't want you to feel you owed me anything. That wasn't the way I wanted things to be between us.'

'Instead of which Max broke the news to me and made everything a thousand times worse,' she said ruefully. Her anger had gone now and she was feeling more her normal self.

'You'll keep the part?' Daniel sounded anxious.

'Yes.'

'That's a relief.' He grinned. 'I wasn't sure how far your high principles might take you. I was beginning to worry about my investment in the production. I can't afford to lose money hand over fist, you know.'

'I'll do my best to see that you get a fair return,' she promised him lightly. 'That's if Max doesn't kill the play on the first night with one of his shattering criticisms.'

'Let him try,' Daniel laughed. 'This show's going to run for ever or I'll know the reason why!'

'Don't count your chickens, Daniel,' she warned him.

'Rubbish. I'm right, you'll see.'

And, as the final rehearsals took place and they set out on the road for the six-week tour that would lead eventually to the West End, Vanessa began, cautiously at first, then with growing confidence, to share his optimism. It was going well, everyone agreed. The first audiences received the play rapturously and the pattern continued during the next weeks. Local press notices were uniformly enthusiastic and most of them singled Vanessa out for the greatest praise, noting the sympathy that she built up for her character and the skilful way she put over her doubts and fears.

In many respects it was not a difficult part to play. Vanessa found it easy to identify with the girl that she was representing. She knew all too well how deep and hurtful love could be when it turned sour. And she knew about rejection enough never to want to risk it again. Love wasn't worth the pain it brought, she told herself.

She did not feel sociable and held herself slightly aloof from the other members of the cast, although they would have been friendly enough if she had let them. Instead she spent her days wandering around on her own, inspecting what the various towns they visited had to offer. She toured art galleries and museums until her head span with culture. She looked at shops. When the weather was bad she stayed in her digs and read anything and everything. It passed the time until the evening when she headed for the theatre with a sigh of relief. These days she only really came alive when she walked on the stage and took on the character of someone else.

Daniel visited her when the demands of his office permitted and sometimes, she suspected, when they did not. And, when he couldn't be with her, he telephoned and did everything he could think of to make her feel happy. Flowers arrived for her dressing room in each theatre they went to. Boxes of chocolates and hampers appeared at her various lodgings. She began to feel slightly overwhelmed by the attention.

'You're swamping me, Daniel,' she told him. 'Stop it!'

'It's only because I love you.' The blue eyes that met hers were serious for once. 'You know that, don't you?'

'Yes.' She had been dodging the issue for too long. It was time that she did some straight talking. 'And it's no use—I've told you that.'

'You'll get over Max.'

'Perhaps. But I'll never love you, Daniel. I shouldn't

have gone on seeing you. It was selfish of me to let you hope for so long. I'm sorry.'

'You won't change your mind?'

'No,' she said firmly. 'Leave me alone now, please.'

He didn't try to argue. He could tell that she meant what she said. Without his comforting presence she felt lonely, but she knew she had done the right thing. In a fortnight's time they would be in London, the first night looming ahead of them. There would be no time for brooding then. It would be a good thing for her. She had spent too much time worrying lately. Some time in the future she would get her romantic life back on its usual even keel, without the violent swings of elation and despair that she had suffered recently. Until then, she told herself, her acting came first. Personal feelings were in cold storage.

She heard nothing of Max. She didn't really expect to. Then, one Sunday evening, she joined her landlady to watch the large colour television that was her pride and joy. It was better than sitting in her room reading. Vanessa sat through an American feature film, taking very little in. It was a thriller with plenty of action and twists in the plot and her mind gave up the struggle to work out the intricacies of it all about halfway through.

'Cocoa, dear?' her landlady offered as the film drew to a close. She accepted gratefully. Perhaps it would help her sleep. All too often lately she had still been awake in the small hours, worrying about that all-important first night and the reception that she would get. She knew she was good. But what if no one else agreed? And Max Anderson's assurance that she would never find work again if she didn't reach his standards of excellence hung over her like the sword of Damocles. She shivered at the thought of it all.

Mrs Thompson came back into the room and moved

to switch channels. 'You don't want the news, dear, do you? All that fighting everywhere. Downright depressing I call it.'

'No, I don't mind,' Vanessa assured her hastily. She got to her feet, mug in her hand. 'In fact, I'll be——' She stopped abruptly, the words dying in her throat as Max's face suddenly came into view on the screen before them. Automatically she sank back in her chair again and leaned forward, intent on the programme before them.

Mrs Thompson gave her a curious look, but said nothing. She was too busy devouring Max herself. He was interviewing one of the government ministers about funds for the arts and he made it fascinating viewing. The subject itself could have been as dry as dust under less expert hands. But with Max it came alive.

The man was a slick performer, a clever public speaker who had long since mastered the trick of talking at length with apparent frankness without really giving any information away. He was clever enough to con most people, but Max had his measure instantly. His relentless questioning stripped away the layers of padding and had the man wriggling in his chair and mopping his brow with discomfort as he pinned him down and forced him to give some real answers for a change.

It was an interesting technique to watch when he was using it on other people, less enjoyable if one was at the receiving end, Vanessa imagined. Max accepted no excuses and refused to skate over awkward issues. He was a merciless opponent. The camera lingered long enough on the minister to catch his faint sigh of relief as time ran out and Max had to wind up the programme. It would be a long while before he ventured to embark on a return match.

Max enjoyed cutting his sort down to size. Vanessa remembered the play script that she had typed for him.

It had made fun of just such a bureaucratic blunderer, exposing him with a wicked sense of humour that had been absent tonight. She wondered if Max really disliked the man he had been interviewing just now. A trace of impatience had crept in that was usually absent in his discussions. She had never known anything ruffle his cool manner before. In his professional life, that was, she amended hastily. He had lost his temper often enough with her.

'I do like that Max Anderson. He really does get them going, doesn't he?' Mrs Thompson voiced her approval loudly over the closing credits. 'And he's a treat to look at too. It'll be a lucky girl that lands him.'

Vanessa agreed absently. There was no point in arguing the fact. She went to bed instead and lay there restlessly trying to sleep and failing. Max's face refused to be banished from her mind. It was over a month ago that he had stalked arrogantly away from her at the press reception, not allowing her to utter a word in her defence. In that moment she had hated him as she had never hated a man before. She had thought of him often in the last few weeks, although she had made a conscious effort not to. Somehow a chance word or phrase, sometimes even an idea loosely expressed, had the power to conjure his dark features into her mind.

And tonight she had only to see his flickering image on the television screen for the hatred that she thought she felt towards him to disappear and all the old longings revive and intensify. It didn't matter that he despised her as an actress and a woman. All she wanted was the feel of his arms around her, the touch of his lips against hers. What fool had said that physical feeling died after a while? If her experience was anything to go by, exactly the opposite was true.

What was he doing now? How was he managing without her? With his usual competence, she supposed.

There would no doubt be a queue a mile down the street when he advertised the vacant secretarial post. And every one of the applicants madly besotted with him and overwhelmed at the idea of working for the man who had stunned them on the television. She absolved him from enjoying that kind of adoration; he hated being stared at as a public face. Vanessa smiled at the thought of his irritation. At least she had never embarrassed him by admitting that she loved him, although she had come near to admitting it that night at Jill's flat.

The lucky girl who was his new secretary would have a rude awakening when she started working with him. She would discover that his temper was diabolical, his standards were exacting and his presence disconcerting to say the least. But perhaps she wouldn't mind. Maybe she would cope better than Vanessa had done. No one could manage any worse. Of course it probably helped not to be in love with the man.

Fortunately the next two weeks passed in a hectic blur that left no time for reflecting on Max Anderson. There were too many other matters to fill Vanessa's waking hours. The first night was four days away, then three, and suddenly it had arrived and she was sitting in the star dressing room in a state of flat panic. Her dresser was fluttering around her making last-minute adjustments to her first act costume, the tannoy on the wall was registering the subdued buzz that was the audience settling itself into its seats, and then there was the assistant stage manager's voice cutting in to summon all those who were due on stage as the curtain went up.

Vanessa licked her dry lips. Why had she ever wanted to become an actress? Why hadn't she taken up something safe and dull like chartered accountancy? Why hadn't she decided to earn her living almost any other way than by going out on a stage in a few minutes' time and making a complete fool of herself? She looked at the pile of good luck telegrams that littered the dressing table in front of her. There was a lucky black cat made of pipe cleaners that Jill had sent her. There were flowers all over the place. People she thought would have forgotten her long ago had remembered her.

And she wasn't going to let them down this time. This play was not going to be a repeat of *Pontoon*. She was going to be a success. Her heart nearly failed her when she thought of Max sitting out there in the stalls with the other critics, waiting to review her performance. It was a bit like being an early Christian thrown to the lions, she decided. But at least the Christians had a sporting chance. Or did they? She was past thinking any more. What was her first line? She couldn't remember it. She had a ghastly feeling of blankness, utter panic.

Then someone pushed her along the narrow corridor that led from the dressing rooms to the stage. The glare of the lights was somehow warm and comforting. She was amongst friends. The butterflies in her stomach fluttered and then calmed as she said her opening words. It was going to be all right.

The interval applause was encouraging, but it wasn't until the final curtain that they knew for sure. The silence from the audience in the last harrowing moments of the play was intense. Then the deafening roars of approval that rang out from all sides of the house signified that they were a success.

'Look at that,' one of her co-stars said out of the corner of his mouth as they took their bows. 'Even some of the critics are clapping.'

Vanessa wondered if Max was one of them. Probably not. It wasn't his style. She looked, but she couldn't see him anywhere. There were shouts of approval as she took a solo bow and renewed bursts of clapping kept the curtain rising and falling steadily. It was almost as if the audience couldn't bear to let them go.

'What did I tell you?' said Jonathan as he sat in Vanessa's dressing room a quarter of an hour later, a glass of champagne in his hand and an expression of deep satisfaction on his face. 'You've done brilliantly, my girl. I knew it from the beginning. This play couldn't fail. Didn't I say so?'

'Yes, Jonathan,' Vanessa agreed obediently. He'd said just that about *Pontoon*. But tonight wasn't the time to think of her failure in that. She was an assured success now. Her dressing room was overflowing with people who were only too anxious to tell her so. Some were friends; some were people she had never met in her life before. Still others were familiar faces from the worlds of television and films.

And they were all congratulating her, Vanessa Herbert, on a stunning performance! Was she dreaming this, she wondered, as a casting director who had definitely no time for her two months ago fawned over her with promises to be in touch with her about a new television play that would, he assured her, be exactly right for her. Vanessa looked across at Jill who was sitting quietly in a corner letting the whole scene swim before her. She didn't believe it was happening either.

The tide of people continued for quite some time and soon Vanessa's face ached with receiving congratulations with a grateful smile. Daniel appeared as if from nowhere and caught her to him, kissing her full on the lips.

'I thought you were in the States?' Since she had rejected him he'd gone back to New York. She had had a brief card from him. Tonight he had sent her a good luck telegram and a large bouquet of flowers.

'I wanted to keep an eye on my investment,' he told her. 'I snuck back yesterday specially for the first night.'

He had a girl with him, a slim blonde who seemed nice enough. 'I'm glad to see you're not that broken-hearted,' Vanessa said softly to him.

'Caroline, you mean? A passing fancy.'

'Like I was?' she asked him teasingly.

'You were never that,' he told her. 'If I thought there was a chance that you——'

She kissed him on the cheek. 'There isn't.'

'Sure about that?'

'Quite sure.'

Her dresser came in at that point like a guardian angel, determined to rid the place of all these people. 'Come along now, everyone out! Miss Herbert has to change for the party.'

There were a few grumbles, but they were good-natured ones. In the space of a few minutes Vanessa had the place to herself. Her dresser had helped her out of her costume and had left her alone. 'You'll be glad of a quiet moment or two to yourself after all that mob,' she said cheerily, and Vanessa had agreed.

She reached for her wrap and put it round her, then began the automatic process of creaming her face to remove the heavy stage make-up. Her head was spinning with all the noise and excitement that had surrounded her since curtainfall. That must be over an hour ago, she thought in surprise as she looked at her watch. She felt suddenly weary, as if she had been dragged off on a ten-mile hike. She supposed in a way that she had been. The strain on her nerves this evening had been tremendous.

Now that she was alone her thoughts went to Max. He had been out there somewhere in the darkened auditorium. What had he thought of the play? Had he liked it? More important, had he liked her? What kind of notice could she expect from him tomorrow morning? It was a long time to have to wait. She wondered if he would eat his words about her and admit that she had acted well tonight. Not for him the massively inflated praises that the other critics sometimes indulged in. If he thought something was good, he said so bluntly, not in a high-flown way. That always made his good opinion worth having.

She roused herself from her reverie and reached for her dress. There was a party at one of the big hotels to celebrate the play's success and she would be expected to attend. Jonathan had already whisked Jill off there in his car, arranging to meet her later. Daniel had gone on ahead too, although he had offered to wait around to drive her there. She had refused the invitation with a smile at the girl with him, who was looking a little disappointed. She wanted him to herself, and who could blame her?

'I'll get a taxi, thanks,' she told him. 'I'll be ages yet, what with changing and messing around. You don't want to hang about when you could be enjoying yourself. Just make sure they keep some champagne for me, will you?'

He didn't try to force the issue. 'You bet! I'll save you a whole case full.'

Vanessa did her face and hair with care, then slipped into the evening dress and pulled it up over her shoulders. It was a slinky black outfit that clung to every curve and looked daringly seductive. It had been more than she had expected to pay, but somehow it had seemed made for her and she hadn't been able to resist it. She zipped it up and studied herself in the mirror with critical eyes. She presumed, without false modesty, that all eyes would be on her when she finally arrived at the party. It was as well to ensure that she looked at least presentable.

She yawned as she got to her feet and took her coat down from its hanger. She supposed it was ungrateful of her to be thinking like this, but she would much rather be going home to the flat and seeking her well-earned bed than dancing the night away in celebration. The penalties of fame, she thought, and laughed aloud. What an idiot she was sometimes!

Everyone else seemed to have gone already, she noticed as she made her way through the empty, echoing corridors to the stage door.

'You're the last one to leave, Miss Herbert,' the stage door keeper told her in some surprise. 'I thought you might have gone out the front way. I'm afraid all the autograph-hunters have given up long ago. Still, you won't mind *that*, I'm sure.'

'No.' Sometimes it was an effort to pin on a smile and sign her name for the fans when all one really wanted to do was go home as quickly as possible. But it was still a sufficiently new sensation for Vanessa that she had enjoyed it on the whole so far. Tonight, however, it would be a relief to dodge it. 'Goodnight,' she called, and stepped out into the street, shivering as a blast of cold wind howled round her. She wondered whether she should step back and ask the stage door keeper to get her a taxi, then decided not to bother. Shaftesbury Avenue was only round the corner and she wouldn't have any trouble in attracting a cab at this time of night.

She was walking briskly out towards the main street when a tall figure stepped out of the shadows and came over to her. For a second she felt uneasy. After all, it was late and the area wasn't that salubrious for a woman on her own.

'Hello, Vanessa.'

She would know that voice anywhere. Her heart started the usual wild dance that Max Anderson always induced in her. 'Hello,' she managed feebly. 'What are you doing here?'

'I phoned my notice in and came back. I've been waiting for you.'

She supposed there were a lot of witty responses to that, but she could only ask directly, 'Why?'

'I wanted to talk to you.' His voice was as cool as ever. It sent shivers of attraction down her spine. One would never have guessed from his manner that this was the man who had flung away from her with such loathing only a few weeks before.

Well, she could be cool too. 'Really?' she said, achieving a note of faint surprise. 'I thought you said all you wanted to say the last time we met. I understood I wasn't to have the pleasure of communicating with you again.'

'You haven't lost that sharp tongue of yours in the meantime, have you?'

'Did you hope that I might have?'

'No such luck,' he said, and there was an odd note in his voice that she couldn't immediately identify. 'We can't talk here,' he went on with more familiar impatience. 'I've got the car parked round the corner. You're heading for the party, I suppose. I'll drive you there.'

Vanessa opened her mouth to refuse and then shrugged. What was the point in being childish about it? He was probably going to the same place. And she couldn't resist the thought of a few moments alone with him, whatever the consequences. She let him take her arm and lead her towards the car.

She was silent as he switched on the ignition and edged his way out into the main street. She studied his features for a clue to his mood and drew a blank. He didn't seem over-eager to talk either now that he had her to himself. She cleared her throat nervously. 'What did you want to speak to me about?'

The car drew to a halt at a set of traffic lights and then surged ahead in a sudden burst of speed. At first she thought he hadn't heard her question and was going to repeat it when he answered her. 'Daniel tells me you're in love with me,' he said in a conversational tone. 'Is it true?'

Vanessa had expected anything but that. A comment on the play, perhaps, or her performance in it. Even a reference to some shortcoming of hers in the past that had caused him inconvenience. But never *that*.

'Well?' he pressed her. 'Was he right?'

'It's nothing to do with you,' she told him desperately.

'It's everything to do with me, if it's true.'

'It's not,' she lied. Heaven forgive her, but she couldn't take his ridicule.

In the light of the street lamps she saw a sudden frown crease his forehead and wondered if he believed her. Did it matter one way or another to him? The car raced forward as he trod on the accelerator. Vanessa was suddenly aware that this was a very long journey to a hotel that was a short distance from the theatre.

'Where are we going?' she asked him. 'Where are you taking me? They'll be expecting me at the party.'

'They can expect,' he said carelessly. 'I'm taking you to the flat. We've got quite a lot to get straight between us.'

'There's nothing I want to talk to you about,' she told him furiously. 'I hate you, Max Anderson!'

'You've told me that before. Women who repeat themselves bore me.'

'You don't have to put up with me. Turn the car round and take me back to the party.'

'Later,' he said imperturbably.

'You can't just abduct me!' she protested.

'Can't I?' he asked, faint amusement creeping into his voice. 'I thought I'd done exactly that.'

'I'll be missed.'

'I told Daniel you'd be with me. He'll make your excuses for you.'

'Daniel seems to have volunteered quite enough on my behalf already,' she snapped. 'Anyway, it's up to me whether I accompany you or not, and I prefer not.'

'What are you going to do about it? I wouldn't recommend you to make a jump for it. You'd only break your neck going at this speed.'

'A fat lot you'd care!'

'You'd be surprised,' he assured her, and she subsided back in her seat, aware that there was nothing that she could do to alter the situation, however much she disliked it.

By the time they drew up outside the apartment block where Max lived she had had time to think. She didn't know what was going through his mind, but she mistrusted the look of devilry on his face. There was danger ahead, of that she as sure.

'I'm not coming in with you,' she said firmly. 'If you won't drive me back to town, I'll get a cab from here.'

'You will get out of the car, walk through that door and into the lift with me,' he told her. 'Or, if you prefer, I can carry you. It's less dignified, but you never have bothered about that, have you?'

He meant what he said, she could tell. She got out of the car, contemplated the possibilities of sudden flight and dismissed them instantly. He would catch her before she had got fifty yards, probably well before then. She would have to do what he wanted. She stalked ahead of him to the lift and stood silently by his side until it reached the top floor. Then she got out and waited by his door while he found his keys and opened it for her.

She walked into the living room, switching on the lights as she went. Nothing had changed as far as she could see. The desk by the window was still piled high with papers. Whoever was working for him wasn't making a very good job of it. She had organised things a little better.

For some reason the familiar territory unnerved her. She had meant to remain silent, let him make the first move, but something impelled her to talk. 'How—how did you get on with the play?' she asked. 'Did they take it?'

'Yes.'

She swallowed nervously. 'I thought they would. It was very good, you know. Very funny. Very witty, I mean.'

'Yes, I know.' Max wasn't helping matters, lounging by the door, looking wickedly attractive in his dark evening clothes. Vanessa felt the pull of attraction that always drew her to him and forced herself to ignore it. 'So you're launched on a new career now. Television dramatist, no less. How will you fit it all in?' She was babbling incoherently and they both knew it.

'Shut up, Vanessa,' he told her.

'Why?' she faltered.

'Because I want to kiss you,' he said and, taking a quick couple of strides across the distance that separated them, he took her in his arms and bent his head towards hers.

'But you hate me,' she protested.

'And you hate me. So we're quits,' he said. And then his lips stilled further protest on her part.

She was trembling when he finally let her go. 'Vanessa, I want nothing more than to take you into the bedroom and make violent love to you, and I suspect that you feel the same way. But there are explanations to be made that are long overdue.'

'Do they matter?' she asked. All that she cared about right now was the sudden miraculous fact that Max wanted her again; that his anger seemed to have evaporated; that he was looking at her in a way that was making her head swim.

'I love you,' he said.

'Is that by way of explanation?' she asked, bemused.

'More of an excuse.' He drew her to sit by his side on the sofa, cradling her against him as if he could not bear to let her go. 'I didn't want you to get to me,' he went on. 'You were everything I despised—or so I thought. And I'd been fooled like that before. I wasn't going to be taken for the same ride twice.'

Vanessa remembered Daniel's story of a girl who had left him for a better offer. 'What changed your mind?' she asked.

'You did. You were different from the other women I saw. You answered back. You didn't just take everything I handed out. You made it clear that you didn't give a damn. You had me wondering if I was on my head or my heels.'

'You didn't do a bad job of concealing the fact,' she said tartly.

Max pulled her towards him, holding her closely. 'I gave you a hard time. Can you blame me? I knew what you were, but it didn't matter. I wanted you anyway. At first I thought it was just a physical attraction. Later I realised that it was much more than that. I let you leave your job with me. I thought a clean break was the best thing.'

'So did I,' she admitted. 'You were affecting me in much the same way.'

'I couldn't stop thinking about you. When I heard the news about your part in the play, I told myself how right I was to get away from you. But I wanted to see you again. I could have sent someone else to that reception. But I wanted to see you. You were a little gold-digger who was playing Daniel for a sucker, but I didn't care. I wanted you. But something drove me on to insult you.' He laughed briefly. 'Afterwards I told myself it was my sense of self-preservation. I've been in hell ever since. I forget the number of times I've set out to come and see you, only to turn back because I wasn't sure how you'd receive me.'

'*You* weren't sure?' She was incredulous.

'Daniel brought me to my senses in the end. I think he fancies his chances as a matchmaker. He told me the truth about you—unsullied virtue throughout.' He ruffled her hair lovingly. 'And, if I wasn't a blind fool, I'd have seen it long ago.'

'You'd have found out, if Daniel hadn't phoned and interrupted us that night at my sister's flat,' she told him.

The tawny gaze kindled at the memory. 'I wanted you that night, Vanessa. You don't know what it did to me to leave you.'

'I've a fair idea. I wasn't exactly happy about it myself,' she admitted.

He kissed her again, dragging his lips from hers with obvious effort. 'I'll make it up to you for that night and all other times I've hurt you. I promise you, Vanessa.'

She pulled his head down towards hers again. 'You could make a start right now,' she invited him. 'That is, if you've nothing better you'd rather be doing.'

'There was some talk of a party.' The devils danced in his eyes as he looked down at her.

'So there was. They'll be sitting round waiting for the early editions of the papers to read the reviews.' She smiled impishly at him. 'I wonder what Max Anderson had to say?'

'He said that you were stunning and that he couldn't take his eyes off you,' Max told her. 'He admitted unreservedly that he was wrong about you first time round.'

'That was very handsome of him.' She smiled up at him. 'I wonder how I can thank him.'

'I think I know a way,' he said. And, swinging her up in his arms, he carried her to the other room.

Harlequin® Plus

A LOVE STORY OF LONG AGO

The literally rags-to-riches story of Nell Gwyn has been a favorite of British storytellers for more than three hundred years. What follows is a sketch of that tale—all we have room for!—but perhaps you will be intrigued enough to research this fascinating historical figure on your own.

"Pretty, witty Nell," as she came to be called by all whose lives she touched, was a child of the slums, poverty forcing her to sell oranges and, by the time she was fourteen, herself. But soon she left the streets behind and took up a career as a stage actress.

It was at the age of seventeen that she caught the fancy of Britain's dashing King Charles II—noted for his extravagances, self-indulgence...and his many love affairs. The King was utterly charmed by Nell's high spirits and exquisite beauty, and it wasn't long before she became his mistress; since any mistress of the King was highly regarded, she, and the two sons she eventually bore him, were well provided for. She was adored by courtiers and the poor alike, for what distinguished her from the King's other inamoratas was her sharp wit, kind nature and generous heart.

That the King loved her in his way, there is no doubt; that she loved him is proven by her faithfulness to him for seventeen years, until his death in 1685.

Discover the new and unique

Harlequin Category-Romance Specials!

Regency Romance
A DEBT OF HONOR
Mollie Ashton

THE FAIRFAX BREW
Sara Orwig

Gothic Romance
THE SATYR RING
Alison Quinn

THE RAVENS
OF ROCKHURST
Marian Martin

Romantic Suspense
THE SEVENTH GATE
Dolores Holliday

THE GOBLIN TREE
Robyn Anzelon

A new and exciting world of romance reading

Harlequin Category-Romance Specials

Available wherever paperback books are sold, or send your name, address and zip or postal code, along with a check or money order for $3.00 for each book ordered (includes 75¢ postage and handling), payable to Harlequin Reader Service, to:

Harlequin Reader Service

In the U.S.
P.O. Box 52040
Phoenix, AZ 85072-9988

In Canada
649 Ontario Street
Stratford, Ontario N5A 6W2

CR-1R

Take these 4 best-selling novels FREE

Yes! Four sophisticated, contemporary love stories by four world-famous authors of romance FREE, as your introduction to the Harlequin Presents subscription plan. Thrill to **Anne Mather**'s passionate story BORN OUT OF LOVE, set in the Caribbean.... Travel to darkest Africa in **Violet Winspear**'s TIME OF THE TEMPTRESS.... Let **Charlotte Lamb** take you to the fascinating world of London's Fleet Street in MAN'S WORLD.... Discover beautiful Greece in **Sally Wentworth**'s moving romance SAY HELLO TO YESTERDAY.

Harlequin Presents...

The very finest in romance fiction

Join the millions of avid Harlequin readers all over the world who delight in the magic of a really exciting novel. EIGHT great NEW titles published EACH MONTH! Each month you will get to know exciting, interesting, true-to-life people .... You'll be swept to distant lands you've dreamed of visiting .... Intrigue, adventure, romance, and the destiny of many lives will thrill you through each Harlequin Presents novel.

Get all the latest books before they're sold out!
As a Harlequin subscriber you actually receive your personal copies of the latest Presents novels immediately after they come off the press, so you're sure of getting all 8 each month.

Cancel your subscription whenever you wish!
You don't have to buy any minimum number of books. Whenever you decide to stop your subscription just let us know and we'll cancel all further shipments.